LETHAL CORRUPTION

JANE M. CHOATE

D0348594

LOVE INSPIRED SUSPENSE
INSPIRATIONAL ROMANCE

LOVE INSPIRED® SUSPENSE
INSPIRATIONAL ROMANCE

ISBN-13: 978-1-335-72291-1

Recycling programs for this product may not exist in your area.

Lethal Corruption

Copyright © 2022 by Jane M. Choate

This edition published by arrangement with Harlequin Books S.A.

For questions and comments about the quality of this book, please contact us at CustomerService@Harlequin.com.

Love Inspired
22 Adelaide St. West, 41st Floor
Toronto, Ontario M5H 4E3, Canada
www.LoveInspired.com

Printed in U.S.A.

"Stay still."

Black lace edged Shannon's vision. She struggled to clear it.

"Are you all right?" Rafe asked.

"I think so. What about you?"

He didn't answer but rolled off her.

It was then that she saw the gash on his face. "You're bleeding."

"It's nothing."

"'Nothing' doesn't bleed like that."

"I said it's nothing. Leave it." A layer of ice coated every word, and she shrank from them. From him.

"I'm sorry," he said. "I didn't mean to scare you."

Shannon got to her feet. A wave of faintness had her wobbling.

"We need to get you checked out and report this."

How had the perpetrator gotten into the building after hours? It was locked down at night, with security people at every entrance. No one got in without proper ID, yet the same thing had occurred when Shannon had been attacked in the lobby.

The implications were chilling.

Jane M. Choate dreamed of writing from the time she was a small child when she entertained friends with outlandish stories complete with happily-ever-after endings. Writing for Love Inspired Suspense is a dream come true. Jane is the proud mother of five children, grandmother to ten grandchildren and staff to one cat who believes she is of royal descent.

Books by Jane M. Choate

Love Inspired Suspense

Keeping Watch
The Littlest Witness
Shattered Secrets
High-Risk Investigation
Inherited Threat
Stolen Child
Secrets from the Past
Lethal Corruption

Visit the Author Profile page at LoveInspired.com.

Blessed is the man that endureth temptation:
for when he is tried, he shall receive the crown of life,
which the Lord hath promised to them that love him.
—*James* 1:12

To teachers.
You are heroes and heroines every day.

ONE

Recycled air from the building's vents huffed ineffectually against the lingering heat of a late August night. The courthouse of Shadow Point, Colorado, held on to the late summer heat with a vengeance.

Shannon DeFord, DDA with the district attorney's office, hurried down the steps to the main floor. The ancient elevator moved too slowly to keep pace with her racing thoughts. She had stayed late to get a jump on the coming day's work.

In the lobby, she paused long enough to sweep her hair from her neck and wipe away the sweat that had gathered there, a palpable reminder that her office air conditioner wasn't working—again—and that she hadn't had even a moment to call building repair.

The air stirred behind her, causing her to startle. The hair on the back of her neck stood up. Moments later, an arm reached out to circle her neck in a bruising hold. In a flash, a knife appeared and was poised at the base of her throat.

She forgot to breathe. Terror crawled up her spine, the trace of its cold finger in sharp contrast to the heat she'd complained of only moments earlier. Her skin pinched like it was shrinking on her scalp, squeezing, pressing, crushing, until she wanted to claw at it and tear it away.

"Drop the case against Newton and his men or suffer the consequences." Though muffled, the threat got through loud and clear.

Her assailant tightened his hold, and she glimpsed something dark and menacing on his forearm. He must belong to the gang who had been terrorizing a block of Shadow Point shop owners into paying protection money. The crew was led by Bobby Newton, who was out on bail.

Newton's gang was a nasty group. As the weekly amount grew to exorbitant rates, the tactics to extract payment had become increasingly violent.

Thanks to the courage of one woman who had come forward to testify, Shannon had an indictment against Newton and three others.

Her eyes flashed back and forth as she looked for the night guard. He was nowhere to be found.

She wasn't given time to ponder over that when the threatening voice spoke again.

"Do you understand?"

The sting of the knife punctuated the words, and drops of blood trickled down her neck. The coppery scent of it nearly made her gag. Or was she only imagining the smell? Didn't matter. All that mattered was her survival.

She managed a nod. If she still believed in prayer, she would have been begging the Lord for His protection right now.

If.

"Good." The arm dropped from around her neck, and she stumbled free, falling to her hands and knees on the veined marble floor. "See that you remember it."

Releasing the breath she was still holding, she stayed there for a minute, maybe two, as she struggled not to let out the scream building in her. Her throat hurt with the effort to keep it inside.

Get it together, girl.

After assuring herself that the assailant was gone, she gulped in a breath and stood. Then she pulled her cell phone from her bag and punched in 911. Fingers clumsy, she tried several times before she could get the number correct.

The security guard eventually showed up. He expressed no surprise or concern when she told him what had happened. "Been on a bathroom break. You look all right to me."

"Thanks." She wasn't a favorite in the police department after prosecuting one of their own for accepting a bribe. Apparently that disfavor extended to the security guard, as well.

A nasty thought occurred to her. Could he have been in on it? Making certain she was alone when the attacker showed up? But how could anyone know when she'd leave her office? Right now, she had more questions than answers.

Forty-five minutes later, a police unit showed up. She made a point of checking the time on her phone. "I thought 911 calls received priority."

"They do. Your call must have gotten lost in the shuffle." The older of the two officers smirked at her, letting her know her call hadn't been lost at all.

They took her statement. Their bored manner indicated that they knew exactly who she was and had little, if any, interest in finding the person who had attacked her.

"We'll keep you posted." He snapped his notebook closed.

"You do that." She didn't bother to mask the sarcasm in her voice.

"You'd best be careful, Ms. DeFord," the younger officer said, speaking for the first time. "Lots of bad stuff going on. Wouldn't want you to get hurt or nothin'."

"I appreciate your concern."

The gloves were off. "You took the badge of one of ours." The first officer's voice was as hard as the nightstick he shifted from one hand to the other. "You won't find much sympathy from the rest of us."

"The blue wall," she murmured. "Too bad it's misplaced in this case."

She didn't give them time to answer, but, instead, turned on her heel and walked away. Why couldn't they see that protecting a bad cop tainted them all with the same brush?

Most of the police officers she knew were good cops, honest and dedicated, but a few had banded together against her, against justice in this case. Her goal had been to prove to them, to the entire city, that no one was above the law.

A gang looting and blackmailing the store owners thought exactly that—that they were above any law. That could not stand. Not on her watch.

In another hour she was in her cozy Craftsman-styled house. It needed work—a lot of work—but it was in a decent area and within walking distance of a shopping center.

If she'd kept her job with the private law firm, she could have had her pick of luxury apartments. Every now and again, she wondered if she'd made the right choice of taking the job with the DA's office then remembered the empty feeling of working solely to make rich people richer. There was nothing wrong with that, but she'd wanted more. Needed more. She wanted to make a difference in the world. She couldn't do that working corporate cases.

Her decision had cost Shannon her fiancé, who claimed he'd proposed to a corporate lawyer, not a lowly deputy district attorney. It was then that she'd accepted that he'd been attracted to a big paycheck and all the perks that went with working for a prestigious company rather than to her.

A week after that, when he'd asked for his ring back, she'd told him that she'd sold it and given the proceeds to her favorite charity, a cat-rescue organization. The look on the face of this man who couldn't abide animals, especially cats, had been priceless.

Despite the heat, she'd taken a hot shower and pulled on a fleecy tracksuit. Gooseflesh peppered her skin as she recalled the cold metal of the knife pressed to her throat.

She touched the wound on her neck, which she'd covered with a small bandage, and admitted to herself that she was as vulnerable as the next person. In response to that, she fingered the gold chain, a gift from her brother, Jeff, that she was never without. It was her touchstone.

Jeff had been her anchor. He had kept her grounded ever since she could remember. When he had been killed while on deployment in Afghanistan, she and God had parted company. What kind of God let a good man like Jeff die? If He was all-powerful, why hadn't He saved him?

Without Jeff, she'd floundered. Only her desire to honor his memory by doing her best had sustained her through the long years of college and law school, when she'd both worked at a fast-food place and gone to school full-time, managing to maintain a 4.0 GPA and to be chosen for the law review.

She'd searched for answers but had found none in the beliefs she'd been taught as a child. The pastor she'd gone to for help hadn't had any answers, either—at least none that made sense to her. He spoke of God's will and submitting herself to it, but she couldn't accept that it was God's will for her brother to die.

Finally, she'd given up seeking answers and had gone her own way. A way that didn't include the Lord. She shook that off and reminded herself that she had a job to do. She had chosen this life, had chosen to prosecute the members of the gang. That wasn't going to scare her away no matter what she'd promised her attacker.

Shannon knew she needed sleep. She also knew that she wasn't going to get any tonight. She was wired. The adrenaline spike following the attack wasn't going away. Work was the only antidote to calm her racing thoughts.

She opened the files and spread them out on her bed. Painstakingly, she went over every statement. One witness, Charlotte Kimball, had been able to recount the men's threats practically verbatim. She would make an outstanding witness.

Shannon wished the other store owners felt the same. They had refused to testify. She didn't blame them. Newton's crew had terrified them, even going so far as to pistol-whip one.

Not for the first time, she wondered why Newton and his men had chosen that particular block to terrorize. The stores were small, the owners mostly older people who made a modest living. They couldn't afford to pay protection money, which Newton had to know.

Money couldn't be the primary reason. There had to be something more, but she hadn't been able to ferret it out. There'd been talk of a new highway going in, but the location hadn't been disclosed. Could that be it?

Was Newton's gang trying to frighten the storeowners away to pick up the properties at bargain basement prices? Whatever the reason they wanted the property, the owners had a right to choose for themselves.

If she failed to secure a guilty verdict, she feared the storeowners wouldn't survive. Their livelihoods would be gone, as well as their homes, since many lived above their shops.

How could they start over after losing everything they'd worked their entire lives for? More importantly, how could they start over after losing hope?

She squared her shoulders and slammed the door on the unaccustomed moment of vulnerability. She wouldn't back down, and she wouldn't back off. She wouldn't be frightened away from doing her job.

Not today. Not ever.

She wasn't her father.

Raphael Zuniga hadn't wanted the protection assignment for the pretty DDA.

Give him an enemy stronghold to take down, a munitions dump to take out or a hostage rescue team to lead, and he was your man. You could take the man out of Delta Force, but you couldn't take Delta Force out of the man.

The rueful acknowledgement reminded him that a soldier's job was to take orders and he took them from Shelley Rabb Judd, a pint-size boss who could be every bit as intimidating as the toughest drill sergeant. It didn't matter that Shelley was two thousand miles away in Atlanta, Georgia, S&J's headquarters.

He'd interviewed with her and her copartner and brother, Jake Rabb, last year and had come away awed at what they'd built. Following that,

he'd spent several months training with other
S&J operatives in Atlanta before taking the job
in his home state.

"Since Gideon's on special assignment, I'm
contacting you directly," Shelley had said, referring to the boss of S&J operations in Colorado.
"Dani's friend Shannon DeFord is in trouble.
Dani says she's good people."

Rafe had listened some more and gotten the
details.

Dani Rabb, Jake's wife, had brought the case
to S&J Security/Protection's attention and asked
for help. One-time college roommates, Dani and
Shannon had kept in touch. When Dani learned
that her friend was being threatened for taking
on a case against a violent crew blackmailing a
group of store owners, and in doing so had put
herself in the line of fire, Dani had asked for
S&J's help in protecting her friend.

It wasn't that Rafe didn't admire what Shannon
was trying to do—he did. It was that he didn't
want to spend his days cooped up in an office.
Give him an assignment that involved action. He
preferred *doing* to sitting any day.

He'd arranged to meet her at the DA's office.
Before announcing his presence, he stood in the
doorway and spent a moment studying his latest
assignment. Medium height, slender, with light
brown hair the color of a fawn's coat, she had

the fresh, wholesome looks of a girl next door. Until you looked closer and saw the purpose in her eyes and the determined tilt of her chin. They promised that she was far more than a pretty face.

He stepped forward. "Ms. DeFord? Rafe Zuniga."

She stood and held out a small hand. "Thank you for coming, Mr. Zuniga." Her office was ruthlessly organized, with only a single file and a lap top on the desk. "I'm afraid I overreacted when I told Dani what happened, and she and Shelley did the same when they asked for your help."

"Shelley said you were attacked here in the building, that someone held a knife to your throat."

"That's right." She folded her bottom lip beneath the upper.

He had a feeling she did so to give herself time to collect herself before continuing, so he pretended not to notice the shaky breath she took.

"The cut turned out to be scarcely a nick. When I'd calmed down, I realized that whoever did it only wanted to scare me." She held his gaze. "I don't scare easily."

"There's no shame in being scared."

Her nod was crisp.

"It could have been worse," he said. Unspoken were the words *much worse*.

She shivered, seeming to acknowledge the implication. Her hand moved to her neck. "I know.

But I can't let a threat keep me from doing my job. That's not who I am."

"No," he said, taking in the firming of her jaw. "I can see that."

"I don't want to take your time for what was only a threat." She looked down at her hands, then met his eyes squarely. "And I can't afford S&J's rates."

"It's on the house."

She shook her head. "I can't let you do that."

"You get the friend-of-a-friend discount. Don't worry about the fee right now. We'll work it out." Though he hadn't wanted the job at first, he couldn't walk away from someone needing help. It wasn't in him.

"I know you mean well, but I can't have you trailing around behind me. Part of my job involves interviewing witnesses. One look at you, and they'll take off for the hills. No offense, but you're a bit intimidating." She paused. "Make that a lot intimidating."

He assumed a meek expression. "I'm gentle as a lamb."

She laughed. "And I'm the queen of England."

He angled his head to study her. "Funny, you don't look like the queen. And you don't carry an ugly purse."

"Just a beat-up briefcase."

He'd kept his tone light. Until now. "It's been

my experience that threats like this only get worse. Not better. I'll stick around. I promise not to get in the way."

She nodded. "Okay. I'll figure out a way to pay you." Her lips quirked at the corners "Maybe I can give up lunches and dinners for the next six months."

Her insistence upon paying him was a point in her favor. Not that S&J would take her money, but he liked that she wanted to pay her own way. It said a lot about her. "Doesn't look like you can afford to miss many meals," he said, gaze raking her slender frame.

"I have a fast metabolism." Defensiveness underscored her words. "And I *will* find a way to pay you. That's a promise."

"Stay alive. That's payment enough."

"You're a strange kind of bodyguard."

"Had much experience with bodyguards, have you?"

"Not a lot." Her voice was wry. "Actually, none at all."

"That's what I thought." His eyes rested on her delicate features, framed by soft brown hair, then moved to her slim shoulders, tiny waist and long legs. A pink dress emphasized her femininity. "You look like you ought to be hosting a garden party, not taking on a gang running a protection racket."

Her voice hardened. "I'm not fragile, Mr. Zuniga. And I go where the job takes me."

"Something we have in common."

Shannon hefted her briefcase. "Let's get to it."

"Where're we going?"

"I have an appointment with a witness on the other side of town."

"Why can't the witness come to you?" Despite his feelings about sitting in an office, Rafe would have preferred that Shannon stay in hers, where she would be easier to protect.

She started for the door. "She doesn't have transportation. Easier for me to go to her. Which is what I'm going to do. You can come or not. Your choice."

Though Shannon looked as delicate as cotton candy, she had the tenacity of a Sherman tank— she seemed ready and willing to mow down any and all obstacles put in her way.

He blocked her way.

"I have a job to do," she said, exasperation heavy in each syllable. "Either lead, follow, or get out of the way."

He scoped out the hallway, then took her elbow. "You don't go anywhere before I check it out. Got it?"

She gave a smart salute. "Got it."

"You have a reputation of being a tough DDA,

but you're looking to prosecute men who would as soon kill you as look at you. Don't be so quick to dismiss what you're up against."

"I don't."

"Good. For my part, I'll keep you safe. That's a promise."

Shannon believed him.

He stretched out a hand ridged with calluses, and tough with the kind of strength that didn't come from a gym but from hard work. It was the hand of a man who put his all into whatever he did. A big part of being a lawyer was reading people. She saw the integrity in his eyes, heard the resolve in his voice. He was a straight arrow.

She had been threatened before. No DDA worth their salt did the job without receiving the occasional threat, but this time felt different. Despite what she'd said to Rafe, she knew that the men behind this weren't playing games. They were serious.

Dead serious.

They made the trip to Mrs. Kimball's shop without incident. The Colorado landscape, with the backdrop of the Rocky Mountains, was beautiful, but even the breathtaking vista couldn't take her mind off the episode with the knife.

Though Shannon had put on a brave act, it

had been tempting to take Rafe's suggestion to stay inside her office. She shook off the lingering fear of two nights ago. Right now she had a witness to prep.

Charlotte Kimball was a prosecutor's dream. At their first meeting, she'd stated the facts without trying to dress them up or down and answered Shannon's questions simply and directly.

"Thank you for seeing me, Mrs. Kimball." She introduced Rafe as an assistant and hoped he would remain unobtrusive. Compared to the tiny woman, he appeared to be a giant.

He gave an infinitesimal nod that he understood and took a seat in the far corner.

They were meeting in the apartment above Mrs. Kimball's gift shop. The store sold pretty but inexpensive items. It had supported the Kimball family for fifteen years and was a mainstay in the close-knit community.

Like the other stores on the block, it didn't have security cameras, something that Shannon sorely regretted. Just one picture of the members of the gang threatening the shop owners would have gone a long way in prosecuting the case against them.

"I wanted to go through your testimony once more." Shannon didn't need the notes she'd prepared, but she took them from her briefcase, anyway.

With only a minimum of prompting, she took Mrs. Kimball through the events leading up to her store being vandalized and her being knocked out. Sincerity and honesty shone in Mrs. Kimball's eyes as she answered the questions Shannon put to her.

The woman put a hand to her cheekbone where a bruise marred her skin. "Then they hit me. Out of pure meanness. I can't think of any other reason."

Such was her anger at the men who had hurt Mrs. Kimball that Shannon wished she had them in front of her now, but she'd bide her time and wait for the court date. It would be easy—too easy—to give in to that anger, but she rejected the idea. Being outraged wouldn't bring her any closer to the justice she sought for Mrs. Kimball and the others. It would only push her closer to the evil she fought. In the meantime, she intended to do everything she could to present the strongest case possible.

It wasn't enough for her to show an unshakable case to the jury. She needed to persuade the members that no one had the right to threaten others.

Charlotte Kimball carried herself with quiet dignity. There was no question that her testimony would not only be well received, but also believed.

Shannon put one final query to the lady, one she would use to close her questioning at the time of the trial. "Mrs. Kimball, would you please tell us why you are testifying when others refused to do the same?"

"Because it's the right thing to do." The words practically beamed with honesty.

"Thank you, Mrs. Kimball." Though it was probably unprofessional, Shannon pressed the lady's hand between her own. "You'll make an excellent witness."

"Thank you."

"I wish we had more people like you."

Mrs. Kimball deserved to be able to operate her store and live her life without fear. Shannon was determined to get that for her and for every other person who had been bullied by the crew.

She didn't blame the other store owners for being unwilling to testify against the men who had ruthlessly torn apart their places of business and made vile threats against anyone who spoke out against them, including their families, but she couldn't help but compare them to this courageous woman who was doing her part because it was the right thing to do.

The country needed more people like her.

"Is it true that a highway may come through here someday?" Mrs. Kimball asked.

"There's only a rumor," Shannon said and prayed for the shop owners' sakes that it wasn't true.

"I can come get you the day of the trial," Shannon said.

Mrs. Kimball smiled. "No need to put yourself out. I'll take the bus."

"Together, we'll stop these bullies and make things right. That's what they are. Bullies." She tried the word on for size and decided she liked it.

"'Make things right,'" Mrs. Kimball repeated. "I know you can do it. I hear the fire in your voice, see it in your eyes."

Making things right was the reason Shannon had become a lawyer in the first place.

"Thank you, again."

Mrs. Kimball rose. "We do the best we can. That's all we can do."

"I'll see you in three days."

"I'll be there."

Shannon had no doubt of that.

"She's quite a lady," Rafe said as they exited the building.

"She is that. She volunteered to testify when no one else would."

"I'm guessing you have protection on her."

"Yes, but not enough. The police complain that they're already stretched too thin." Shannon gave a wry smile. "I'm not the police department's favorite person right now, not after I prosecuted one of their own."

Outside, she shaded her eyes from the sun and gazed around the block that had seen too much violence. *It stops now.*

A woman jaywalked across the street and bustled between Shannon and Rafe.

A roar of sound cracked the air.

Shannon didn't react immediately. When she did, her breath came in short hard pants that seemed to rob her of all thought.

Rafe pushed her to the ground. "Gunshot. Stay down."

Shannon watched the woman fall, as though in slow motion, as blood blossomed on her pretty blue blouse.

Another shot pierced the air. Shoppers, who had been strolling along the sidewalk only moments earlier, screamed and scattered.

Shannon started to scrabble her way toward the woman.

Rafe held her in place. "I said stay down."

"That woman…she needs help. I need to—"

Rafe shut her off with a fierce look. "Don't you get it? That bullet was meant for you."

TWO

"I'm sorry. We can't give out information to non-family," a nurse in pink scrubs said when Shannon asked about the woman who had been shot.

Rafe had known they wouldn't be able to get any word about the woman by going about it this way. He figured Shannon knew it, too, but she'd insisted they come to the hospital, anyway.

Now she turned to him, eyes pleading for him to understand. "I had to try."

He was learning that that was who she was, and admired her for it, but it ramped up the difficulty of protecting her. A second shot had quickly followed the first. Fortunately, no one else had been hit, but it emphasized the danger his client was in.

His patience was on a tenuous leash.

First, he and Shannon had had to make statements to the black-and-white units. Then they'd had to repeat the same thing to a detective who'd shown up. Now, they were in the waiting room of the hospital, where he was chafing at the knowledge that Shannon was once more making herself a target.

The shot had come from a high-powered rifle, probably a .22 Hornet. He was familiar with the weapon and knew that it was designed to kill with maximum efficiency. The knowledge that someone had used the weapon against Shannon iced his blood. When was she going to accept that she had a bull's-eye painted on her back?

As though in answer to the question, he patted his own weapon holstered at his shoulder, a Heckler & Koch P7 handgun. He'd liked the H&K submachine guns he'd used in Delta and used the equally reliable P7 for his personal weapon. The H&K was a meticulously machined German gun. It hadn't let him down when he'd been in Delta. It wouldn't let him down now.

Voices—some strident, some tearful, some worried—filled the room, mixing with the undercurrents of antiseptic and despair. He did his best to block them out, but they seeped through despite his efforts.

Rafe hated hospitals.

Having spent the better part of a year in various hospitals and a rehab center, first for the treatment of his wound, then to learn how to use his prosthetic leg, he hated the smells and sounds of both. The pungent odor of cleanser and the beeps and whistles of monitors called up night-marish memories. And, worst of all, the air was thick with despair and the fragile hopes of those waiting for news of loved ones.

He pulled himself from the painful memories and focused on the here and now. He had a job to do—keeping Shannon safe. So far, he was batting zero. Though the hospital had security, it wasn't enough to keep a determined shooter from setting his sights on Shannon again.

He hadn't been able to persuade her from coming to the hospital, but enough was enough. He took her elbow and steered her to an exit. "We're going."

Unsurprisingly, she resisted. "I need to find out how she's doing. We can wait for her husband to come out. He'll be able to tell us."

"Why should he?" Rafe asked bluntly. "We're strangers to him."

"Because—"

"We'll find out, but we aren't going to learn anything here," he said. "Not now."

"You're right. I know about HIPAA and all of that, but I had to try." She flushed. "I already said that, didn't I?"

Hearing the concern in her voice, he softened his own. "I'm sorry. I know you're worried about her. So am I."

"She was shot because of me."

He wouldn't let Shannon shoulder the blame. "No. She was shot because some lowlife wanted to kill you. You aren't responsible."

"I wonder if her husband feels that way."

He stopped, turned to her and faced her. "It won't help her or her husband for you to blame yourself."

She nodded. "You're right. I'm making your job harder. Let's go back to the office."

Rafe made multiple SDRs before being certain that they weren't followed. Surveillance detour routes could be tedious, but they made it possible to identify a tail, enabling them to make the trip to her office without incident.

He parked in a lot adjacent to the office, where they were less likely to be noticed, but didn't get out of the truck. Instead he looked at her, saw the desolation in her eyes. She needed to forget the pain and ugliness of the last few hours, if only for a moment.

"Best first date ever," he said, straight-faced.

He was gratified when she laughed. The job had just gotten a lot more interesting.

Shannon was still smiling over Rafe's words. There had been little to smile about in the last few hours, between an innocent woman taking a bullet meant for Shannon, giving the statements to the police and making a futile trip to the hospital. He had given her a reason to smile, and for that, she was grateful.

It didn't, however, make his security precautions at every step easier to swallow. While she appreciated what he was trying to do, she was growing tired of the extreme safety measures.

At her desk, Shannon went over Mrs. Kimball's testimony and her own opening statement. *Again.* No detail was too small to overlook. She made more notes, checked and double-checked her facts and wondered if there was more she could be doing. It didn't escape her notice that she had three other cases pending, though they were for relatively minor offenses. No one at the DA's office had the luxury of working on only one case.

Rafe's presence was a distraction, though he didn't move from the sole visitor's chair. He appeared to be engrossed in a worn paperback and didn't clutter the silence she prized so highly with meaningless chatter.

When her phone rang, she answered eagerly. She was expecting a call from a colleague about another case.

"You've been warned."

The voice had been electronically altered. With nothing more, the call was disconnected.

Rafe looked up. "Tell me."

She repeated the three words.

He took the phone from her, checked the number. "We can put a trace on this, but I don't expect we'll get anything."

The call had jolted her, but she snapped back to reality. "Another scare tactic. Nothing to get upset about." Who was she trying to convince? Rafe? Or herself?

The rest of the afternoon was spent working on her other cases, including contacting the involved officers. Some proved cooperative; others did not. She wasn't surprised and accepted it for what it was.

Dinnertime came and went, but she scarcely noticed, having switched her attention back to her primary case. After hours at her desk, with a headache pounding at her skull, she was ready for a break.

When Rafe suggested they get something for dinner, she nodded.

"You look like a strong wind could blow you over. You need to eat. What's more, I'm a growing boy and I'm hungry."

Taking in his six feet four inches and muscular build, she laughed. She packed her briefcase, closed and locked the door behind them and let Rafe check out the hallway before she ventured from the office. It was as empty as it often was when she left for the day.

Dinner turned out to be burgers from a fast-food place. Rafe vetoed the idea of eating there and they decided to return to her office.

"We need to talk," Rafe said as he drove back to the courthouse. "Newton and his gang won't go down easy. You have to know that."

"Of course I do." Impatience shimmered in her words. "He's denying the charges. And he has plenty of friends who'll stick up for him. The judge granted bail, so he's out on the street. I mean to make sure he stands trial and that he and his crew spend a long time in prison."

She paused and took a long breath before continuing. "I can't let them win." Her voice grew louder with every word. She could never tolerate those who used superior strength or size to hurt others. To her, it wasn't just a matter of principle. It was saying that no one has the right to abuse others, whatever their station, whatever their circumstances.

Without realizing it, she was saying the words aloud. "Sorry. I didn't mean to lecture you. If I'm to nail Newton and his band of merry men to the wall, I need to make sure I have all my geese in a row."

"Don't you mean ducks?"

"No. I mean geese. Geese are much more independent. That means I have to work that much harder to corral them then teach them to stay in line."

"You have a point there."

Inside the building, he inspected the elevator, then they rode the car up to the twelfth floor, where the DA's offices were located. "Stay here until I check out the office."

Taking orders never went down easy for Shannon. Taking orders from a man who issued them with total certainty that they would be obeyed without question went down even harder.

"You're my bodyguard," she said between gritted teeth, "not my boss. So stop acting like it."

"And you're the one who has a target on your back. When I say 'stay here,' you stay here. Got it?"

He turned, and she had the childish impulse to stick her tongue out at his back.

Rafe Zuniga was supremely confident. Of course, why shouldn't he be? With a Delta Force background, he exuded strength, courage and integrity—all of which she admired. At the same time, she wished he would stop treating her like a child.

He returned. "There's a tote bag on the floor that I didn't notice earlier. Pink and purple. Is it yours?"

She shook her head and started to go in the office.

He grabbed her arm, halting her progress, and

showed her the bag propped at the corner of the desk. "Who does this belong to?"

Tension whispered in the air.

"It's probably Eve's," she said, naming the legal secretary who liked brightly colored accessories. "She must have come back, then accidentally left her bag here."

His gaze sharpened. "You've never seen it before?"

"Well, no. But that doesn't mean anything. It's not a big deal. She'll get it in the morning." A faint ticking, like an old-fashioned clock that was slowly winding down, distracted her.

Rafe must have heard it, too, because he grabbed her hand and ran. They made it to the central hallway before an explosion rocked the office.

THREE

The air around them hissed and snapped, the noise reverberating. She shook her head in an attempt to dislodge the sensation in her ears of someone filling them with stuffing then pulling it out. It didn't work. Her nostrils burned and her eyes stung from the acrid smell in the air.

Debris had landed on them, but she didn't dare move. As though to add emphasis to that notion, there was a heavy weight—Rafe—pressing her against the floor.

Rafe!

Was he all right? He'd shielded her body with his own. She tried to turn her head to see if he was all right.

"Stay still."

Rafe's voice.

Black lace edged her vision. She struggled to clear it.

"Are you all right?" he asked.

"I think so. What about you?"

He didn't answer, but rolled off her. Shannon tried to sit up, found that the black lace curtain intensified when she moved. She put a hand to her head in a futile attempt to stop the dizziness.

"Lie still," he said, gently pushing her back.

It was then that she saw the gash on his face. "You're bleeding."

"It's nothing."

"'Nothing' doesn't bleed like that."

"I said it's nothing. Leave it." A layer of ice coated every word, and she shrank from them. From him.

"Sorry," he said. "I didn't mean to scare you."

Shannon got to her feet. A wave of faintness had her wobbling.

"We need to get you checked out and report this." The grimness in his voice echoed her own thoughts.

How had the perpetrator gotten into the building after hours? It was locked down at night, with security persons at every entrance. No one got in without proper ID, yet the same thing had occurred when Shannon had been attacked in the lobby.

The implications were chilling. She pushed them aside for now.

Rafe picked her up as though she weighed no more than a doll and carried her to a chair outside the range of the blast. Being in his arms was unsettling, a sensation she did her best to ignore.

"You don't need to carry me."

"It's no trouble."

"I know." But it was. The trouble lay in her feelings when her unwanted bodyguard held her. The disquieting knowledge sent her thoughts into turmoil.

"Stay here and catch your breath. I'll be back in a few minutes."

She didn't protest. She needed time to let her heart stop galloping in her chest and return to its normal rhythm. The meditation exercises she'd started last year came in handy.

Breathe. One, two, three...

Slowly, her muscles relaxed, the tension leaving with every breath.

When Rafe returned, she got to her feet, albeit a little unsteadily, and met his gaze without flinching. "How bad is it?"

"Your office is pretty much trashed, along with the cubicles next to it. Who knew you'd be working late?"

Her brow wrinkled in thought. "It's no secret that I often work late." A frown pulled at her lips when she recalled the weird way the security guard had acted when she'd been attacked in the lobby. She mentioned that to Rafe now, and added, "He'd know when I left the building earlier."

"So your secretary would know along with anyone else who works here." He didn't give her time to answer. "Someone knew. Whoever did this could have slipped the bag in here while we were out picking up the food."

Another chill chased down her spine. Had someone she knew, someone she worked with, set her up and tried to kill her?

The EMTs arrived, checked them out and treated the gash on Rafe's face. If it had been up to him, he'd have slapped a bandage on it and called it good. He and Shannon both rejected going to the hospital.

Rafe didn't like the glazed look in Shannon's eyes. Shock. He'd seen it often enough in Afghanistan, especially among new recruits. For many people, violence existed only on a news channel. No one accepted that it could happen to them.

Even Shannon, who prosecuted cases on a regular basis, didn't fully accept the reality that someone wanted her dead. How could she remain so naive after everything that had happened to her?

"We'll be down to the station tomorrow and

give our statements," Rafe told the detective who'd shown up.

"Tonight's better."

"I want to get Ms. DeFord home. She's in shock."

The detective followed Rafe's gaze to take in the unnatural paleness of Shannon's face. "All right."

Rafe didn't bother answering. He needed to get her home. She'd been hurt on his watch. The knowledge ate away at his gut.

She gave him directions. After that, the trip to her place was made in silence. The ambient light from the dashboard cast everything in shadow. He glanced over at Shannon and saw that her eyes were closed, her eyelashes creating dark crescents beneath. She looked unbearably fragile, as though she would break at the slightest bump. She was pale enough that he imagined he could pass his hand right through her.

His hands gripped the steering wheel harder as he thought of the men who had done this. If he had his way, they wouldn't stand trial at all. He rejected the idea right away. That wasn't the Lord's way, but his anger was such that he had actually considered it, if only for a moment.

Be still, and know that I am God. The scripture from Psalm 46:10 soothed away some of the ragged edges, and he gave silent thanks to the

Lord for always being there and keeping him on a straight course.

When he pulled to a stop outside her home, she woke. "I'm sorry. I didn't mean to drift off like that."

"You're entitled."

"Thank you for what you did tonight. You saved my life."

It had been close. Too close. He should have realized the danger far earlier.

He ignored her insistence that she could walk to the house on her own.

She didn't take the arm he offered, but when they reached the front door, she asked, "Can you stay for a while?"

He needed sleep and had intended upon calling a female operative to stay with Shannon overnight, but he couldn't say no to the appeal in her eyes.

"Sure."

"I'll make hot chocolate. It always makes me feel better."

"Sounds good." He'd have preferred a cold pop, but Shannon needed the comfort of hot chocolate.

Once they were settled at her kitchen table with steaming mugs of hot chocolate in their hands, he asked, "Why did you take this case? You had to know it could be dangerous."

Shannon didn't answer directly. "This gang

has brutalized more than a half-dozen shop owners. They threatened their families, including elderly parents and small children." She shivered.
"I can't imagine anything worse than knowing
your family is in jeopardy."

A frown crept into her eyes, and he wondered
if she was thinking of her own.

"Where are your parents?"

"They split up when I was ten. Neither one
wanted a kid around cramping their style when
they started dating other people." Though her
tone was casual, the shadows in her gaze held
more than a hint of sorrow.

"You mean they abandoned you?" He wasn't
able to keep the disbelief from his voice. Though
he and his mother didn't always agree, she loved
him and his sisters.

"My brother stepped up. Jeff was in college,
but he came home and took care of me, made
sure I got to school, did my homework, went to
the dentist. All the stuff parents are supposed
to do. Eventually, he got legal guardianship of
me. When I was old enough to start college, he
enlisted, even though he was older than the average recruit. He said he wanted to make a difference in the world." She drew a shaky breath.
"He died his first year of deployment."

"He sounds like a good man. About your
parents—"

"They're out of the picture, like I told you."

Out of the picture but not out of her heart. What must it have been like to have her parents desert her that way?

Shannon shook her head, as though to wipe away any sympathy he might feel. "It doesn't matter. Not now. What matters is that we stop Newton and his gang. They're no better than common bullies. That can't stand." Her slim shoulders squared, making her look bigger than she was.

"I get it." Rafe knew it *did* matter, but he went along with her change of subject. Like Shannon, he could never tolerate those who used superior strength or power to hurt others. It wasn't just a matter of principle, it was criminal behavior on the part of Newton and his gang. No one had the right to abuse others, whoever they were, whatever their circumstances.

He'd witnessed horrific things during his time in the military. None of those sights, though, had sickened him more than cruelty toward children. As one of his buddies had said, such acts hurt him in all his soft places.

By the end of his tour, Rafe hadn't believed he had any soft places left, but one incident had reached down and squeezed tears from his heart when he'd thought he was unable to shed another. An insurgent had used a small child as a shield.

Seeing one of the world's innocents used by the enemy that way had enraged him to the point that he'd risked his life to save the child, then taken out the enemy with his bare hands.

"You're a tough lady."

She shook her head. "Not so tough. I sat by and let you deal with the police tonight. I should have been the one answering the questions." She clamped her hands together. After she gazed down at her locked hands, then looked up, her eyes were hard. "I got their message. It's time they got mine. I won't be scared off from doing my job. Not like…"

"Like your father."

"You know?"

His nod was brisk. "Your father was Lynwood DeFord, an ADA fifteen years ago. He dropped a case because he was being threatened."

"Go on. Say the rest of it."

"He did more than drop the case," Rafe said, not pretending to misunderstand. "He took money from the man he was supposed to be prosecuting."

"The technical term is 'malfeasance.' He made his choices." Shannon's voice hardened, but he heard a faint crack in it, as though she was struggling to keep her composure. "Just like I make mine. I won't be scared off." A little pause. "I can't."

"Like I told you before—there's no shame in being scared. Only a fool wouldn't be afraid in these circumstances, and you're no fool."

"Thanks for that, but don't you see? If I drop this case, then I'll never be able to trust myself again."

"You're not your father."

"I know."

"Just don't let it cost your life proving it."

"You'll keep me safe." She sounded sure of it. "You promised."

She had him there. "And I'll do my best to keep it, but your enemies have already made three attempts on your life. What's going to happen when they try again? And they will. Make no mistake about it. They will."

At that moment, a spasm of phantom pain shot down his leg. The idea of pain in a missing limb had puzzled him at first. Now he accepted it and was learning to live with it.

"Your leg's hurting," she said.

"Yeah. Some. The leg's not there, but it still hurts. The doctors called it phantom pain."

"I've heard of it. Can you tell me about it?"

"You want to know how I lost my leg?"

"If you want to tell me."

Strangely enough, he did. "My unit was on patrol. We had reports of the enemy in the area and wanted to confirm them. On the road back to headquarters, we hit an IED." He swallowed deeply, then continued. "Our vehicle was cut in half. Two of the men died immediately. Another man was thrown clear. I was knocked out. When I came to, I was in a portable hospital with half my leg gone."

He didn't go into detail. There was no need to burden Shannon with the fear and pain that had warred within him, each seeking dominance as he struggled to wrap his mind around the fact that he was missing half his right leg. "The doctors there did the best they could, then shipped me home. I spent the next year in and out of hospitals and rehab."

"You're remarkable."

"Hardly," he said. "It was the Lord who saw me through it."

The certainty of his faith reminded her that she'd once been a believer. When Jeff had been killed, her faith had died along with him.

"I'm better off than many who came home," he continued, "missing two legs, or arms and legs, or traumatized so badly that they couldn't function in the outside world. IEDs don't discriminate.

"I did my stint in therapy and was discharged from the army. I knew I needed to do something. I also knew I couldn't work in an office. I'd heard about S&J overseas, how they hired special operators. I've been with them for the last year. They're the best."

"Thank you for sharing that with me. It couldn't have been easy."

"No. It wasn't. But it felt good."

Shannon yawned. She clamped her hand over her mouth and gave an embarrassed smile. "Sorry."

"Don't be. You've had a long day. Go to bed."

"What about you?"

"I'll bunk here on the couch."

She looked doubtful. "Are you sure?"

"Don't worry about it. Get some sleep. Something tells me that you're going to need it."

After she had retreated to her bedroom, Rafe settled on the sofa, knowing he wasn't going to get a lot of sleep. Not because of the sofa. He'd slept in worse. Far worse. In a desert where the heat crawled up his back only to pour down it in sweat. Beneath a canopy of leaves in a steamy jungle with his head tucked against his chest as rain beat down without rest. In the back of a military transport jet, strapped to the seat with his head bobbing up and down.

No, sleep didn't depend upon comfort, but on the release of tension. Why had he told Shannon about losing his leg?

He didn't share that period of his life with many, but somehow doing it with Shannon felt right. And that worried him. It meant he'd let down carefully erected barriers.

It didn't make sense—they'd known each other for less than a day—but he didn't doubt that the Lord had put Shannon in his life for a reason.

Some people thought he would give up his belief. What kind of God, a friend had asked upon visiting Rafe in the hospital, allowed a soldier defending his country to lose a leg? Rafe had answered that the Lord had spared his life and asked only that he make the best of his new one. His friend had shaken his head and walked away. Even some of the nurses and doctors had questioned his devotion to God.

Far from having his faith shaken, Rafe had doubled down on his belief, knowing that it was the Savior who had seen him through the worst time of his life. Just as He had seen him through the excruciating pain of learning to walk again with a prosthetic leg.

Rafe had refused to feel sorry for himself. Instead, he'd found a job with S&J and a new purpose: helping people in trouble, like Shannon. Knowing that he was able to do what he was born to do—fighting the world's bullies—kept him sane.

"I'll take care of you," he said, though Shannon wasn't there to hear. A wave of protectiveness washed over him.

He had to step up his game. Someone had gotten close enough to plant a bomb in Shannon's office. That should never have happened, and, if he had anything to say about it, it wouldn't happen again.

Bring it. And with that, he drew a line in the sand.

FOUR

The precinct station was in full swing at 8:00 a.m. Detectives with their sleeves rolled up and suspects with hands cuffed behind their backs bickered in sometimes loud, sometimes bored voices.

Phones rang.

Computers hummed.

Printers beeped.

The occasional shout and even a scream here and there punctuated the buzz of constant voices.

All in all, it was a cacophony of sound that did nothing to defuse the pounding in Shannon's head. The pungent odor of coffee that had sat too long mixed with the unrelenting smell of pine cleanser in a losing battle with vomit and worse.

Shannon was accustomed to the sounds and smells of the station house. What she wasn't accustomed to was the knowledge that she was there as a victim rather than as a representative of the DA's office.

Victim.

Instinctively, she rejected the word. She cringed inside at the idea that she was being referred to in that way and clamped down on her tongue to keep her outrage inside. No one here cared that she flinched every time she heard the word.

Bile rose in her throat, the acid burn of it causing her to gag and mocking her determination to hold up and hold on.

With what seemed like superhuman effort, she forced down the bile. Getting sick in the police station would destroy her rep as a take-no-prisoners DDA. She was no one's victim and wouldn't allow herself or anyone else to think of her that way.

She briskly answered the detective's questions, kept her head high and steadied her voice. When it quavered over a word, she pressed on. Rafe's occasional nod of approval bolstered her courage.

The detective took her statement, leading her through the events of the evening. "I'm sorry to say so, but you're a target, Ms. DeFord," he said at the conclusion of the interview. "You were wise to have hired a bodyguard. We'll do our best to keep you safe, but our department is spread pretty thin."

When she raised an eyebrow, he flushed, and she guessed he was thinking that there were some among the police who wouldn't mind seeing her injured.

"I know that some of our people haven't been cooperative with your office, but that's about to come to an end." His eyes hardened. "I have nothing but gratitude that you pulled a corrupt cop from our ranks. Most of our men and women are fine officers, but now and again, we get a bad apple."

"Thank you, Detective."

"Be cautious," he said and hummed a little while he made notes. "In the meantime, we'll try to trace the few components of the bomb that are still intact. Maybe they'll lead us to whoever set it."

His voice told her that he didn't expect results. Neither did Shannon. Building a bomb was alarmingly easy these days. Instructions for it could be found on the internet with only a few keystrokes.

"Thanks for coming by." He bent his head over a sheaf of papers, effectively dismissing the two of them.

Rafe took Shannon's arm and steered her outside.

"I refuse to be a victim," she said as he drove to her office.

"I hear you. But there's no shame in being a victim."

"But that's not who I am." Her words had taken on a shrill note. In a quieter voice, she said, "It's not who I want to be."

"You don't have to be strong all the time."

"You're saying it's okay to be weak once in a while?" She shook her head in answer to her own question. "I can't let up. For one thing, this case is too important. For another, if I show weakness, the rest will circle like sharks."

"The rest of whom?"

"The others in the office. When I was promoted over a couple of them, they saw it as favoritism on the boss's part. I don't see it that way, but I'm not going to apologize for doing my job well." She'd had to fight for her place there and had done her best to ignore the petty remarks of coworkers.

"They don't know you at all." The certainty in his voice was backed up by the steady look he sent her way.

She sent a grateful look his way. "No, they don't."

"I thought you said that no one else in your office wanted the case."

"They don't, but they'd love to see me fail. Even better, become a victim of the men I'm supposed to be prosecuting." She gave a small shrug. "It's human nature."

"You sound pretty accepting of it."

"You get used to it. But I won't play the victim card. And I won't be run off."

"There's a difference between courage and foolhardiness," Rafe said. "Newton won't go down easily."

"I represent the justice system. When someone abuses that system, I tend to take it personally."

"And the attacks on you? Do you take them personally, as well?"

"I can't afford to. If I did, I'd never be able to try another case."

Despite her brave words, she couldn't deny the nerves that had her jumping at her own shadow once they were in the office. Fear was a weight that clamped down on her energy, her resolve. How could she uphold the principles that had always defined her if she allowed panic to turn her skittish?

With workmen there to repair the damage done by the bomb, she had to get over jumping at the slightest noise. Hammering and banging seemed to be the order of the day. The glares some of her coworkers directed her way told her that they blamed her for the damage to the office.

What was she supposed to say? *I'm sorry that someone tried to kill me by setting a bomb?*

They would think what they wanted to. Her responsibility was to the people who had been terrorized by Newton and his crew. She would get justice for Mrs. Kimball and the others. If she couldn't do that, then she didn't belong in the DA's office.

For the rest of the morning, she did her best to focus on the job, but she wasn't fooling Rafe... and she wasn't fooling herself. She was running scared.

"It's okay," Rafe said in a quiet voice. "You could step down from the case."

She glared at him. "No way."

The corners of his mouth turned up in a satisfied smile, as though that's what he'd wanted her to say. "Good. You've got your sass back. You put me in mind of my grandpappy."

"Your grandpappy?"

"Yep. He used to say that some people were as stubborn as a Missouri mule."

"Seriously? A Missouri mule?"

"Seriously."

"I don't believe it and I don't believe you called your grandfather that."

"I might have exaggerated a bit," he admitted.

While she enjoyed the banter, she had to bring the conversation back to what mattered. "I will bring those men to justice. Newton and his crew aren't as smart as they think they are."

"What do you mean?"

"If I'm hurt or killed, someone else will take

over. The DA's office doesn't give up a case just because a DDA is taken out."

"How long will it take another attorney to get up to speed?"

She chewed on her lower lip. "A couple of weeks, at least. Probably more like a month."

"Anyone else going to volunteer to take the case?"

"I get where you're going with this. But none of it changes the fact that the DA's office will eventually put Newton and his men on trial. It may be later rather than sooner, but they'll be brought to justice, one way or the other."

"A lot can change during that time," he pointed out.

"Are you trying to get me to back down?"

"No. Just trying to make you see what's at stake here." He paused. "Namely, your life."

"I can't help that. If Newton and his crew get away with this, there'll be no stopping them. They think they're above the law. I aim to show them—and everyone—that no one is above the law."

Before he could continue the argument, she was summoned into the big man's office.

Not nearly as tall as Rafe, Hamilton Brooks made up for it with a powerful build—he was thick in the shoulders and chest. His rolled-up sleeves revealed tough forearms and he wore a Perusia watch on one wrist.

She respected and admired him and, if she was honest, feared him a little. He wielded power, not only in the DA's office, but also in city hall and beyond. But she was grateful to him for bringing her on board at the DA's office. Here, she was making a difference in the world, far more than she had made while working in her previous job.

More than one member of the staff had expressed doubt about hiring her, but Brooks had maintained that Shannon was a team player who wouldn't let down him or the office.

She'd done her best to prove him right and had tackled every job, large or small, with single-minded resolution. Though she'd lost a few cases, her win-loss ratio remained on the positive side. It wasn't the score, though, that mattered. Not to her. It was the knowledge that she was helping make the city she loved safer for everyone.

"You wanted to see me?" she asked.

A big smile stretched across his jowly face, but something in his eyes didn't match up. Or was it only her imagination that detected a flicker of disapproval there?

He didn't speak right away, and she spent the time waiting by glancing around his office. It was utilitarian, as was to be expected of the district attorney, with only two things hanging on the walls.

A plaque with the words *citius venit malum quam revertitur*, a new addition to the office, caught her attention. Though her law-school Latin was rusty, she translated the words as "evil arrives faster than it departs." The only other decorative touch was a framed award for shooting.

Something tickled a memory, but she couldn't identify it.

"I'm glad to see that you're all right. I heard about last night. Seems like you've put yourself in the line of fire several times over the last few days."

That wasn't how she'd describe it, but she nodded. "I survived." Her attempt at humor didn't elicit a chuckle, as she'd hoped. More seriously, she said, "I didn't exactly *put* myself in the line of fire. The crew we're after did that."

He clicked his pen several times before putting it down. "No one will blame you if you step aside on this, DeFord. In fact, there might be another case that would better showcase your talents."

"I'm sorry?" Had he just suggested she drop the case?

"You've proved yourself here. You can take a pass on this one—let someone else take over. When I assigned it to you, I thought you were the right person for the job, but..." He cut off whatever he'd been about to say as though thinking better of it. "You're too important to this office to become a target."

"If I step aside, wouldn't that make someone else a target?"

He waved a hand, dismissing the idea. "Things might change."

She kept her voice even, though she wanted to throw the offer back in his face. "Thank you for the suggestion, sir, but I'm okay. I've already done the legwork. It would take time to bring someone else up to speed. And time is something those shop owners don't have."

"Think about it. Take a day or two. I'd hate to see you get in over your head."

"I don't run." Her voice took on a hard note.

"I know that," he said, impatience sliding under the concern. A pinched scowl now took the place of the smile he had worn earlier. "But maybe it's time you stepped back, let someone else take the lead."

He was annoyed with her. She could see it in the rigid set of his shoulders, the heaviness of his breathing, the twin lines of frustration between his eyebrows.

"If you think I'm not pulling my weight—"

"It's not that," he said, his scowl tightening. At the same time, a muscle in his jaw twitched. He ran his fingers through the comb-over that failed to conceal a growing bald spot.

Everyone in the office agreed that he would be better served if he cut the hair and left the bald spot, but no one, including herself, had had the nerve to say so. The result was that long strands of his hair stood on end, making her think of the picture of Einstein that had hung in her eleventh-grade science room.

"You know that a lot of people in this office thought I'd made a mistake in bringing you on board. Some of those same people thought I'd made another mistake in giving you this case. I did it because I thought you were ready for it. Now…" He paused and steepled his fingers together. "I'm not so sure. The office is getting a lot of the wrong kind of publicity because of you."

"You're blaming me because some lowlife decided to play rough?" Shannon stopped herself before she said that that wasn't reasonable or fair.

"I'm not blaming you." His irritation spiked again. "Just watch yourself, okay?" What had caused the bleak expression to cross his face? She wanted to ask but instinct told her to leave it. Her boss wasn't a touchy-feely kind of guy and wouldn't appreciate the personal question.

"I'll be safe. I have a bodyguard who makes sure of it."

"I heard about him. From S&J Security/Protection, isn't he?" He nodded. "They have a good rep."

"Yes, they do." She turned to go.

"One more thing."

"Yes?"

"I want you at tonight's bash. Bert Calhoun is pulling out all the stops. I want my people there in a show of support."

She didn't have to ask which "bash" he was talking about. Albert "Bert" Calhoun, owner of the state's biggest construction company and a major player in local affairs, was throwing a fundraiser for Brooks, who was running for governor.

Brooks had made it clear that "his people," as he called them, were there to make him look good. It irked Shannon more than a little that she was expected to show up for the affair when she had so much work to do.

"Sir, with all due respect, I wasn't planning on attending. I have three other cases pending, aside from the Newton one, and I—"

"Be there. That's an order." He smiled, no doubt an attempt to remove the sting of his command. Too bad it didn't work.

"Yes, sir." She did her best to keep the resentment from her voice. Judging by the scowl he sent her way, she hadn't succeeded.

"Shut the door behind you. I'll see you tonight."

Outside his office, she closed the door and leaned against it. Just what she needed—a summons to a black-tie affair. She had enough work to keep an office of DDAs busy, the beginnings of a headache and nothing to wear.

It was the last problem that she needed to address immediately. For her previous job, she'd had a number of evening gowns for the formal events she was required to attend, but when she'd left the law firm, she'd sold the fancy clothes at a consignment shop. The extra cash had come in handy for rent and food.

Rafe was waiting for her in her office. "What's up?"

"He wanted to know how I was doing." It struck her as more than odd that Brooks had suggested that she hand off the case to another member of the office. "And to give me an order to attend the fundraiser tonight."

"The fancy to-do at the Regency?" he asked, naming the city's number-one hotel.

"You know about it?"

"My mother is big in the city's social scene. Tonight's hoedown is all she's been talking about for weeks."

Despite her irritation with her boss, Shannon

grinned. "'Hoedown'? I don't know if I've heard it described quite that way before."

His eyes crinkled with amusement. "Probably not."

"Frankly, a hoedown sounds like more fun." Dress-up affairs weren't her style. She'd take a night of pizza and pop with friends anytime over a fancy party where gossip and bad food were consumed with equal fervor.

Backtracking to something Rafe had said, she realized he'd never mentioned his family before. "Tell me about your mother."

"My mother was my biggest cheerleader when I was doing rehab. She wouldn't let me get away with not doing everything I could to walk again. If I started feeling sorry for myself, she asked if she should bring cake to the pity party. I owe her a lot." He paused, then added, "We usually get along great."

Shannon picked up an offbeat note on the word *usually*. "You said 'usually.' Does that mean you're not doing so great right now?"

Rafe drew his eyebrows together until there was scarcely a space between them. "We aren't on the best of terms at the moment. She wanted me to take over the family business last year when my father died."

"The family business?"

"Allcott Mining." The words seemed pulled

from him as though that was the last thing in the world he wanted to admit.

Shannon gave a low whistle. Allcott Mining was one of the biggest mining operations in the state, perhaps the entire West.

"But your name—"

"When I got back from Afghanistan, I took my mother's maiden name so that people wouldn't make the connection. I don't need everyone knowing that I'm Jason Allcott's son."

She got it. "You didn't want others to see you as 'heir to the throne.'"

"Something like that. Don't get me wrong— I loved my father. But I'm not a businessman. Nor do I want to be. The idea of sitting behind a desk…" He shook his head. "That's not me."

"Does anyone else know?"

"My boss, Gideon Straham, knows, but he keeps it to himself." His mouth quirked in a lopsided smile. "I can hear the ribbing I'd take at work if the others knew I was billionaire Jason Allcott's son."

"You don't act like you're rich." She flushed. "I'm sorry. I didn't mean it like that."

"I'm not rich. I don't work for Allcott, and I don't take money for what I don't do. My dad left me an inheritance, but I don't use it. I live on what I make at S&J. That's it." His lips firmed, and he broadened his stance, as though daring her to criticize his choices.

This was another side to the man—a side she liked a lot. The more she learned about him, the more she found to like. She wanted to continue the conversation, but the darkening of his eyes and flexing of his jaw said that he was anxious to put it aside.

Plus, she still had the problem of what she was going to wear to tonight's event. She'd attended only one fancy affair in the time she'd been at the DA's office and had worn a dress she'd borrowed from a coworker. That wasn't an option any longer as the coworker had moved away.

"I have to go shopping."

Rafe raised an eyebrow. "Shopping?"

"My boss seems to think that I have a dozen formal gowns in my closet that I can pull one out at a moment's notice."

"You'd look lovely in anything."

His cheeks flushed, making her wonder if he was as surprised at saying it as she was at hearing it.

Her mind emptied of everything but his words. Though she didn't spend a lot of time on her hair and makeup and clothes, she was woman enough to like hearing a handsome man say she was beautiful.

"C'mon, Mr. Bodyguard. We have to find a

dress, then I have to come back and cram three days' work into an afternoon."

"I don't know anything about shopping for a dress." The look of panic on his face had her insides smiling. The big bad ex-Delta was petrified at the prospect of shopping.

"You're about to learn." She made her tone brisk, but the feelings inside her at his earlier words were anything but brisk. They were warm and gooey, like just-out-of-the-oven fudge brownies.

A stern reminder that warm-and-gooey feelings toward her bodyguard were in no way professional didn't help.

At all.

Rafe decided he should put in for hazard pay. Shopping was a blood sport in the large discount store tucked in the foothills that Shannon had directed him to.

He'd never gone shopping with his mother or sisters—he shuddered at the idea—but he understood enough to know that they patronized stores where suitable clothes were brought out for their inspection while they waited in beautifully appointed rooms and sipped sparkling water.

Not so with Shannon.

She hit the warehouse with fire in her eyes and impatience in her steps. Women of all shapes and sizes and ages fought over garments with a fervor he'd witnessed only on the battlefield. Battle-hardened soldiers who had faced the enemy without flinching would have cowered at the hordes of women who attacked the sales racks in a fevered frenzy.

He reached for a dress, curious as to the price, only to have it snatched from his hands by a lady whose gaze told him to release the garment immediately. Which he did. He'd faced less intimidating heavily armed insurgents.

When Shannon grabbed a dress in dull gold from a large circular rack and headed to a curtained-off cubicle that served as a dressing room, he didn't have much hope that his misery was about to come to an end. The dress looked like a skinny sack that had just been emptied of potatoes. He was the first to admit that his fashion sense wasn't the most refined, but couldn't she have found something better?

Five minutes later, she came out to model it for him. "What do you think?"

He all but swallowed his tongue. When he found his voice, he stammered out, "N-nice."

"That the best you have?"

"Uh…real nice." He couldn't stop staring at her. If someone told him that he was looking at her bug-eyed, he wouldn't have been surprised.

She looked like a vision in the dress, which

was more copper than gold, and skimmed over her slender curves with a gentle hand. The color played up her hair and eyes, giving her a glow that had nothing to do with artifice.

He swallowed. Hard. Not an easy feat when he feared his tongue was hanging out.

She grinned. "That's better. Let me change, then I'll pay for it and we can go."

Ten minutes later, they were on the way back to her office. The entire trip had taken less than an hour, and Rafe was left in openmouthed astonishment that she could choose and buy a dress in that amount of time. If he told his mother and sisters about it, they'd have called him a liar and demanded proof. He loved his family dearly and respected their talents tremendously, but he couldn't imagine them accomplishing such a feat.

The drive through the canyon leading back to Shadow Point was beautiful, with the backdrop of the Rocky Mountains and sky the color of a child's blue crayon.

When he'd been deployed, he'd seen mountains all over the world, from the Swiss Alps, while on a brief furlough, to the harsh skyline of the Afghani mountains, but none compared to those of Colorado, already capped with snow.

As the land temporarily leveled, the foothills gave way to rolling fields of feed corn, their brilliant greens testament to the recent rain and the rich Colorado earth. After he'd returned from Afghanistan, with its relentless wind and sand and extremes of unbearable cold and insufferable heat, the lush scenery of his home state never failed to move him.

The road started to climb again, taking them through a deep canyon.

"You're amazing," he said. "You did in an hour what would have taken my mother and sisters all day to accomplish."

"Let me guess. They go to designer stores where no one glances at price tags and the saleswomen all look like supermodels who haven't eaten in a month."

"Something like that." The defensiveness in his voice mirrored his tense muscles. His mother and sisters did what came naturally to them. Just as Shannon did.

"It sounds…fun." The grimace that crossed her lips said it sounded like anything but fun. "I can't afford that kind of shopping."

He recalled what he'd read about her—that she'd left a prestigious law firm where she made a salary in the high six figures to take the much lower-paying job at the DA's office. "If you'd stayed at your last job, you could have."

She shrugged. "Maybe. But representing rich people whose only goal in life was to get richer wasn't worth it. That isn't why I went to law school." There was that fire in her eyes again, but it was far more intense this time. Passion infused her words—passion and a fierce determination.

"Then why take the job to begin with?"

Determination showed on her face. "To pay off student debt. Four years of college and three of law school add up. I'm still whittling it down, but I can see the light at the end of the tunnel. Barely, but it's visible."

"You're not like any woman I've ever known." That was the truth. Shannon was driven, often impatient and totally dedicated to her job. She was also beautiful, smart and funny. All in all, a potent and appealing combination.

If they'd met under different circumstances, he'd might have acted on the attraction, but she was a client and clients were off-limits. A reminder that several of his coworkers, including his bosses, had fallen in love with and married clients reared its head. He did his best to squash it, but was left with the uncomfortable feeling that it wouldn't stay buried.

Honesty forced him to admit that it wasn't really the job that kept him from pursuing a relationship. He'd been burned before. Badly. He couldn't risk his heart again.

He wouldn't.

"Is that a good thing?"

He was about to say that it was a very good

thing when motion in his rearview mirror caught his attention.

A tractor-trailer was coming up on their rear. It wasn't moving to the other side of the road, as though it wanted to pass, but remained steadily behind them, its speed matching their own. The road passed through a narrow canyon with steep cliffs on either side. Rafe hugged the edge of the road and motioned out the window for the driver to pass, but he didn't take advantage of the gesture.

When he encountered another truck just ahead, he tried to pass it, understanding the game plan. No wonder the first truck had not seemed in a hurry to pass him and Shannon. They were now boxed in on the narrow two-lane highway with no way out. Gravel spit from the tires of the tractor-trailer in front of them, pinging Rafe's windshield. Shots followed.

Rafe pulled his weapon from his waistband, wanting to have it close.

"Keep low and hold on." He did his best to keep his distance from the trucks, but there was nowhere to go.

The road had opened now, one side of the canyon wall dropping away. A steep drop-off took its place.

Shannon's hands clenched in her lap. To her

credit, she didn't distract him with pointless questions but let him focus on what he needed to do.

Rafe's fingers were white-knuckled on the steering wheel. What he did in the next few seconds would determine if he and Shannon lived… or died. Silently, he said a prayer that he would make the right choice.

The narrow ribbon of highway was flanked by a steep cliffside on one side and a sheer rock wall on the other.

He swerved, hoping to squeeze by the second truck, but his maneuver was ineffectual against the momentum forcing his vehicle ever closer to the cliff. With superhuman effort, he forced the wheel in the other direction. He gave the car one final burst of speed, squeaking by the second truck on its right side. Just when he thought they were going to make it, the truck driver pulled sharply to the right so that the heavy trailer rammed into Rafe's car.

He applied the brakes just enough so as to not lose control, then pressed on the gas once more to escape the tractor-trailer as it tried to slam the car again. Rafe veered to the side but was too late. The car flipped, seemed to be suspended in midair for a fraction of a moment, then tumbled down a shallow hill, each bone-jarring bump registering painfully.

With effort, he let his body relax. It was not

easy to do when being bounced around in a car plummeting down a cliff, but a limp body was less likely to sustain injury than a tense one. He tried to shout to Shannon to do the same, but he doubted she heard him over the rough-and-tumble drop as the car rattled and clanged over rocks and scrub brush.

Though the plunging trip down the cliffside felt like it lasted forever, only a few seconds passed before his car came to a halt, landing on its roof. It shuddered for a couple of heartbeats before completely stopping.

Secured by their seat belts, Rafe and Shannon hung upside down. The breath momentarily knocked out of him, he didn't move. When he was able to put two thoughts together, he did a quick inventory for possible injuries and decided he'd live, though his entire body felt like it had been beaten with a baseball bat.

He tried to turn his head to look at Shannon but couldn't see more than her hair and a glimpse of her profile. "Are you all right?"

"I think so."

Her voice shook a little, but the words were clear enough. He had to hand it to her. She hadn't screamed or cried, though he wouldn't blame her if she had. She'd kept her head with as much cool as he'd witnessed among seasoned soldiers.

"Hold on and I'll get us out of here."

He thought she nodded but couldn't be sure. He tried the door but found it jammed shut. With no power, the automatic window wasn't working, so he used the butt of his gun to shatter the glass. Careful of the ragged shards of glass around the window frame, he undid his seat belt and climbed out, head first.

He landed on the ground, which smelled thickly of loam and rotting vegetation. He stood, not surprised to find that his legs were wobbly. A deep breath later, he rounded the car to Shannon's side. The passenger door was stuck, but once he found a large stick to use as a lever, he pried it open.

After he extracted her from the car and carried her a safe distance away, he gave her a once-over. Resolute lines framed her pale face. She would refuse to give way to hysterics.

"You all right?" he asked.

"Fine. Just tell me that the dress survived."

FIVE

What a woman.

They'd narrowly missed being smashed between two oversized tractor-trailers, had been pushed off a cliff and landed with their car flipped upside down, yet she still managed to crack a joke.

He'd have appreciated the humor a lot more if he wasn't worried that the drivers of the two trucks were even now coming after them. His fears were confirmed when a shot came from partway up the hill.

Another shot sounded, this one coming dangerously close to where he and Shannon were standing. Whoever these men were, they'd had sufficient training to shoot with a fair degree of accuracy. As easy as television shows and movies made it appear, hitting a target from a distance was challenging at best.

He and Shannon were sitting ducks. He took her hand and they ran to a copse of pines, but they wouldn't be safe there for long. A nearby rustling alerted him that the shooters were getting closer and not bothering to disguise their pursuit.

The glimpse he'd caught of the driver in the second truck showed that he wasn't wearing a mask, which reinforced what Rafe had figured out: he and Shannon weren't meant to walk away from this.

Another shot sounded, this one coming close to where they were sheltered. From the sound of it, the shot had come from a .22 Comet. Primarily used by the military, the Comet was a powerful weapon designed with one purpose in mind: to kill.

He and Shannon ran deeper into the forest, but the terrain was becoming increasingly more difficult with its boulder-studded ground and scrub pine, and though Shannon was in good condition, she couldn't outpace the men who were chasing them.

It didn't help that they were bracing themselves against a steep ascent. Their breathing grew heavier with every step.

A root as thick as a man's arm sent Shannon sprawling. Rafe helped her up, but when he tried to check out her ankle for injury, she brushed away his hand. "I'm fine. We need to keep going."

When they started off again, she winced. "It's just a twinge. I'll be all right."

They hadn't made it more than a few yards when Shannon's shallow breathing and the white lines bracketing her mouth indicated she couldn't keep it up much longer. He thought of stashing her somewhere safe while he dealt with the two tangos. A grimace crossed his face as he thought of her likely reaction to that plan. There was no outrunning the men. The only other option was to make a stand.

That option was equally untenable. Surely there was another way, a better way. One of the most important rules in taking down an enemy was don't give away what you're thinking. The guys after them undoubtedly thought that he and Shannon would keep running. So they had to do the opposite.

"We need to distract them so that I can get around behind them," he said, thinking out loud. "If I could draw their attention…"

"Let me do it."

"No way." The objection came automatically. "You're the client. You don't get to play bait."

"I can pretend to be injured." She grimaced. "I won't have to pretend much. I'll keep their attention on me, and you can get the jump on them." She voiced the words with certainty, but a hint of nerves coated them, as if they'd got caught just south of her throat.

Of course, she was afraid. Anybody would be.

As a diversion, it wasn't bad, but using the person you were supposed to be protecting as bait wasn't in the S&J handbook. In fact, it was expressly forbidden in case an operative ever had the harebrained idea to try it. "No way."

Shannon cocked her head to the side, where the thrashing of the men through the underbrush was growing louder and closer. The challenge in her eyes confirmed what he already knew: the choices for getting out of here alive were whittling down to somewhere between slim and none. He had his H&K and a clutch piece, but both were puny against the firepower the men were carrying.

He had to make a decision, and he had to do it now. "All right." He prayed he wouldn't live to regret uttering those two words.

The cliffside leveled off, and there was a small clearing. She positioned herself to where she couldn't be missed.

Rafe identified where the men would likely be when they saw Shannon and circled behind. Within a few minutes, their body language showed that they had spotted her. Seeing two armed men advance on her nearly cut him off at the knees. Why had he agreed to this plan?

"Please," Shannon said as the men drew nearer, her voice close to begging. "Don't shoot. I'm hurt."

One man approached with caution. "Where're you hurt?"

The other made a scoffing sound. "Doesn't matter where she's hurt. She's not walking away from this. We got our orders."

She pointed to her right leg, which she held at an awkward angle. "I think it's broken."

If Rafe hadn't known better, he'd have thought the leg was actually broken.

"What happened to the bodyguard?"

"He hightailed it out of here when he saw you coming and knew I couldn't run. Some body-guard, huh?" Disgust was ripe in her voice.

Rafe had to hand it to her. She was playing her part like a pro. Tears hovered in her voice, giving further credence to her plight, and she gave a small moan. "Please, can you help me?"

The larger of the two men snorted. "Lady, you got the wrong idea about us. In case you didn't catch on when we ran you off the road, we aren't here to help you." He guffawed at his joke. He turned to his partner. "Keep an eye on her. I want to check out those trees. I don't trust what she said about the bodyguard taking off, and I don't like surprises." After directing an I-don't-believe-you-for-a-second look in her direction, he disappeared into the brush.

Rafe was steadily closing in from behind. With his Delta training, it wasn't hard to sneak up on the second man and take him out silently with a swift chop to the back of his neck. The blow wouldn't cause any lasting damage, but it would give the man a first-class headache for the next several hours. Rafe dragged him into a thicket of bushes and used the zip ties he routinely carried with him to bind his hands behind his back.

Though he wanted to get Shannon out of there, she insisted she remain in place. "One down, one to go. Do your thing and let me do mine." She preened a bit. "I was good, wasn't I?"

"Real good," he said before he ducked out of sight.

"Pete," the first man called as he returned to the spot. "Where you at?" He glared at Shannon. "Where'd he go?"

"I think he heard something over there." She sniffled a bit and pointed to a spot slightly to the right of Rafe.

When the man went to check it out, Rafe stuck out a foot and tripped him. He fell with a thud, and Rafe dropped to the ground to put a knee on the man's back. "If you know what's good for you, you'll stay down." He used another zip tie on the man's hands.

Shannon scrambled up and dusted off her clothes. Triumph sparkled in her eyes.

Rafe flashed a grin her way and gave her a thumbs-up. "If this gig with the DA's office doesn't work out, you can always take up acting."

"Thanks. It's good to have something to fall back on."

He appreciated her humor, but he knew it had cost her. She'd handled herself admirably, but the lines of strain around her mouth told their own story. Her right hand was shaking, though she did her best to conceal it.

Adrenaline. It had spiked through his bloodstream, as well, his heartbeat slightly accelerating as he'd faced the unknown. He was a seasoned soldier. What must it have been like for Shannon, a civilian, to accept that they'd almost died?

Again.

First, in the car tumbling off the cliffside, then at the hands of the two would-be assassins who'd chased them into the forest. They'd survived this time, but would he be able to keep his promise to protect her against the next attack?

And he was certain there would be a next.

Despite her protests, Rafe had insisted upon carrying her up the hillside. She marveled at his strength as he braced his legs against the steep incline while holding her in his arms as he went.

Though the hill didn't qualify as a real mountain, it came close.

"Do you think the Academy Awards committee will come knocking on my door anytime soon?" she asked.

Rafe chuckled, a pleasant sound that warmed her more than it should have. They had almost been killed—again—and it felt good to hear the rich timbre of his laugh, but the chuckle was cut short by the blare of the arrival of the ambulance.

Shannon had seen more EMTs this week than she had in her entire lifetime. She didn't like it. Didn't like it a bit.

She and Rafe were checked out and deemed to be okay. Her ankle was wrapped and declared a slight sprain.

"You're going to be sore for the new few days," one of the EMTs said, gesturing to her ankle. "Take it easy."

She wished that was an option. "Thanks."

A black-and-white unit arrived on the heels of the ambulance. Rafe explained what had happened and gestured to where he'd left the two men. Within a few minutes, the officers returned, each with a man in tow.

The men shot menacing looks at Rafe and her, shouting what they'd do to them if they ever got their hands on them.

Shannon paid their threats scant attention. Having bad guys promise retribution was nothing new. In fact, if all the people she'd prosecuted who had vowed revenge on her were put together, they'd have made a good-size crowd. The two men being shoved in patrol cars were scarcely worthy of notice.

"Another vehicle down," Rafe said. "I called S&J. They're sending a couple of operatives with a car for us."

"How many vehicles do you normally go through on a case?"

"No more than a dozen or so," he said, straight-faced.

"Good to know."

The banter felt good, but she wasn't forgetful of the fact that whoever had ordered the hit on her was still out there. Taking out the henchmen was good, but she knew it wouldn't stop the real threat. Unless and until they found out who was behind the attacks on the shop owners, she was still a target. She liked the word only slightly more than she did *victim*.

That thought caused her to square her shoulders. She refused to be either.

An S&J operative showed up with a car, with another operative following and driving a second. "The boss says these cars are coming out of your salary," one of the men said, deadpan, to Rafe.

"Tell him he's going to need to give me a raise first," Rafe replied.

After retrieving the all-important dress box

from the wrecked vehicle, Shannon and Rafe drove back to town. The trip was quiet, a relief after the last hour's excitement.

At her office, she immersed herself in her work, barely taking time to eat the lunch Rafe had grabbed from a vending machine and set in front of her. The dry ham-and-cheese sandwich scratched her throat, and the flat pop puckered her lips, but she devoured them, anyway. She needed fuel if she was going to get through the remainder of the day and the night. She didn't expect the fundraiser to have more than appetizers.

As was his habit, Rafe let her work without interruption. For such a large man, he could remain exceptionally still.

Though she wasn't vain, she wanted to spend a little time preparing for tonight and left work at 6:00 p.m. rather than her normal eight o'clock. They stopped at Rafe's place on their way to hers so that he could change into formal clothes.

"I'm impressed," she said when he returned from the bungalow's one bedroom wearing a tuxedo that could only have been designer-inspired.

In a midnight blue tux so dark it was nearly black, and a stark white shirt, he was drop-dead gorgeous, as the colors complemented his deeply tanned skin and dark eyes. Zings of attraction darted through her. She did her best to still them, but they kept reminding her what a compelling-looking man he was.

"A gift from my mother," he said, fingering the lapel of the jacket. "I've never had a need for it, but I can't escort a beautiful woman to a fancy shindig like tonight wearing jeans and a T-shirt."

Rafe would be attractive no matter what he wore. It was easier to reflect on that than on his calling her beautiful. No one had ever uttered those words to her before. Not even her fiancé. She'd been termed attractive, good looking or girl-next-door pretty.

But never beautiful.

No big deal. It was simply a phrase people tossed around, but she couldn't deny the sweet feelings that filled her.

"Do you think I'm beautiful?" Immediately she wanted to yank back the words. "Sorry." She flushed. "That must have sounded like I was fishing for compliments."

"Not at all." He laid the garment bag on a chair and cupped her shoulders in large hands that were oh so gentle. "You are beautiful. You should know that."

She gave a light laugh and slipped from beneath his hands, uncomfortable with the conversation and her response to it. "We'd better get going. I have a little more than an hour to turn myself into a princess."

Something flickered in his eyes but was gone so quickly that she wondered if she'd imagined it.

At home, Shannon spent the next hour preparing for the night's event. In the discount dress and her only jewelry, the necklace her brother had given her, she knew she couldn't compete with the glitz and glamour of the other women who'd be attending, so she went with understated elegance.

She picked out a tiny evening purse and discreet hoop earrings. Her ankle had healed quickly, so she wore strappy shoes with ridiculous heels that would have her feet weeping before the evening was over. After applying some smoky eye shadow and lip gloss, she swept up her hair into a modified twist.

Not bad. The copper-colored dress went well with her coloring. What's more, it hadn't put too big a ding in her bank account.

When she walked into the front room, where Rafe was waiting, his jaw dropped and he stared. "You keep surprising me, counselor."

"I do?"

"You surely do."

"Does that make you my prince?" What was she doing? It sounded like she was flirting with him. That was the last thing she wanted. Wasn't it?

"You've already seen the dress," she pointed out.

"That I have. But it looks different tonight.

You look different tonight." He gestured to the delicate chain at her neck. "I can't help but notice that you always wear this. It must be special."

His tux jacket had opened slightly, and she glimpsed the weapon holstered at his shoulder. The gun served as a reminder of why he was here. A shiver traced down her spine. For the rest of the evening, she decided to put the fact that someone wanted her dead out of her mind.

"It is. My brother gave it to me before he was deployed. He said it was to remind me of him. I never take it off." Her voice caught over the last words, and she coughed to clear her throat. The conversation was turning too personal, and she searched for a change of subject. Though she'd already complimented him on his appearance, she said, "You clean up pretty well, too."

"Nobody's going to notice me. Not when I'm standing by you. I'll just be window dressing."

He couldn't have been more wrong.

It seemed every woman there noticed Rafe Zuniga, she reflected a half hour later as they walked into the sumptuously appointed ballroom. And why not? The dark tux emphasized the breadth of his shoulders and the length of his legs. She tried not to give in to the sin of pride, but she couldn't help being pleased that he was at her side for the night.

Glitter sparkled through the ballroom in the

twinkling lights of chandeliers, the crystal flutes, the jewelry worn by the wealthy patrons. Murmured conversations competed with the clinking of glasses raised together.

Though Shannon avoided such events most of the time, excitement sparked through her at the knowledge that she was here with Rafe. Tonight was work, but she couldn't help wondering if he would ask her to dance. Did she want him to? Silly question. Of course she did.

He answered her unspoken question by leading her onto the dance floor. With his left hand holding her right one and his right hand at the small of her back, he swept her into a waltz. He moved with a lithe grace that had her following his steps without question.

She gave herself up to the pleasure of dancing with him and, for the length of the waltz, blocked out all the fear and tension of the last few days. She was glad she'd worn the heels, ridiculous as they were, because they made her tall enough that she could meet his gaze. His shoulder, warm beneath her hand, was broad and strong and wholly masculine, like the rest of him.

Rafe's breath was warm against her face, and she wished the dance would last forever, or at least beyond the bars of the Strauss melody. The sweet scent of the flowers decorating the room and the soft music played by a small ensemble made the perfect backdrop to the waltz.

"Thank you. That was wonderful," she said at its close.

"I should be the one thanking you. And it *was* wonderful." He moved both his hands to span her waist.

Seconds stretched into a minute, but Shannon and Rafe didn't move. When she realized that they were standing in the middle of the ballroom with hundreds of pairs of eyes on them, she withdrew from his hold and felt the loss. Without his steadying hands, she stumbled backward in the high heels.

Rafe caught her. "Careful in those things," he said and held her once again for the space of a breath before releasing her.

She laughed, grateful that the awkward moment had passed. "My feet are not going to thank me come morning for listening to my vanity and wearing these shoes."

He lowered his gaze to give the heels a critical look. "No. I doubt they will, but I'm still glad you wore the heels."

"You are?"

"It meant I could see your face rather than look over your head."

His words caused a buzz of pleasure to shimmer over her skin. Immediately she rejected that and reminded herself that she didn't need the complications of a relationship. Not now. It wasn't just that her career needed her total focus; she no longer trusted her heart. How could she, when it had let her down in such spectacular fashion in the past?

Having feelings for her bodyguard was wrong on so many levels. She hadn't had a relationship with anyone since her fiancé had deserted her. It had hurt more than she'd wanted to admit, even when she acknowledged that she was better off without him. It seemed every time she cared about someone, they left her. First her parents had abandoned her, then Jeff had been taken from her and, most recently, it was her fiancé.

What made her think it would be any different with Rafe?

In turns both confused by and impatient with her feelings, she seized on the reason she was here tonight. "I need to make the rounds. The boss is expecting to see me."

"Let's do it."

The next fifteen minutes were spent greeting and being greeted by the DA, his wife, others from the office and city hall. Glad-handing was the name of the game, and she did her best to participate in the ritual. The social obligations of the job were among her least favorite parts of working at the DA's office. Fortunately, they happened rarely, so she smiled and made the best of it.

"Shannon, good to see you. Thank you for coming," Hamilton Brooks said, as though she'd had a choice. "You're looking lovely." He grinned, his eyes nearly disappearing into twin crescents above his cheeks. He lowered his voice a fraction. "I hope you haven't forgotten our conversation of this afternoon."

She murmured a thank-you for the first comment and ignored the second. Something was going on with her boss.

She introduced Rafe and noted that he handled the social niceties with the manners of a seasoned diplomat. "You're pretty smooth," she whispered as they moved on.

"Thank my mother. She insisted my sisters and I take etiquette lessons. Believe me, I complained long and loud, but they came in handy when I was deployed. Our unit was occasionally assigned to protect a senator or some other bigwig who always wanted a photo op on the battlefield. Knowing how to keep them safe without offending them was useful. One insisted upon being photographed holding a weapon."

"What did you do?"

"I took out all the ammunition from a rifle, gave it to the senator and told him to pretend to aim it. As it was, he still managed to nearly kill one of my men when he swung it around and hit my second-in-command in the head. My twenty-one-C was all right, but he told me he deserved the Purple Heart." His chuckle was rueful. "Diplomacy is a lot like herding cats. There's little reward, and sooner or later you know you're going to get scratched."

Rafe's story put a smile on her face. She kept it there as she greeted the evening's host, Albert "Bert" Calhoun.

She'd seen pictures of Calhoun before, but up close, he was even more impressive. Power emanated from him. He was a big man with ruddy cheeks and white hair and wore a pinky ring that was as big as one of her knuckles. Something in the ring's design snagged her attention as being familiar, but her glimpse of it was too brief to place, and the kernel of recognition died.

"It's a pleasure to meet you, sir."

He pressed her hand between two meaty ones and led her slightly to the side. "The pleasure is mine, Ms. DeFord. I've heard good things about you. And call me Bert, please."

"Thank you."

"Hamilton is always singing your praises."

That surprised her. Given her boss's reaction to how she was handling the Newton case, she didn't think he'd compliment her work anytime soon. "I owe him a lot," she said.

"I expect to be seeing more of you in the coming months."

"Oh?"

"With Hamilton moving on to the governor's mansion, someone will need to take over the reins in the DA's office. I think that someone could be you."

She shook her head. "Thank you for the kind words but there are others more qualified and with more experience."

"But you have the fire. I see it in your eyes, in the way you move." He winked. "Now, if you'll excuse me, I need to 'press the flesh' for our mutual friend."

"Of course." After excusing herself, she returned to stand by Rafe.

"What did Calhoun want with you?" he asked.

"I don't know." She replayed the conversation in her mind. "I've never met him, but he treated me like we were old friends." Beneath the joviality, there'd been something darker. Probably her imagination.

"That's the way of the big players in town." Rafe gave a good-natured groan and nodded over her shoulder. "Now we're in for it. My mother's on her way."

Shannon turned and gazed at the beautiful woman walking toward them. She looked far too young to be his mother. Impeccably dressed and wearing a gown that probably cost several thousand dollars, the lady stopped here and there to exchange a word, or buss a cheek, but she never lost sight of her goal.

"Raphael. I didn't know you were going to be here. You normally avoid these affairs."

He leaned in to kiss her cheek. "Mother, it's good to see you. I'd like you to meet Shannon DeFord. Shannon, my mother, Monique Allcott."

Mrs. Allcott extended her hand. "I'm so happy to meet you. Raphael rarely introduces the family to any of his friends."

Shannon looked from mother to son and saw the resemblance—the finely chiseled features, the dark hair, the intelligent eyes that were alight with curiosity. How should she answer his mother's greeting?

"Shannon is a client," Rafe said, taking the question out of her hands.

"Is she? I thought… The way you looked at each other…"

Shannon doubted that the lady was rarely if ever disconcerted, but his mother recovered quickly. "Then I take it tonight is business?"

"Shannon works for the DA's office. I'm providing security."

"Oh?" The single word held a question.

"I'm a deputy district attorney," Shannon explained. "He takes after you."

"Really?" Her already beautiful face grew even more so as soft color stained her cheeks. "Most people say he takes after his father, who was also a tall man. But it's nice to hear that you see some of me in him."

"It's plain to me. He has your features."

"Thank you." Rafe's mother gave Shannon a frank appraisal then smiled warmly. "You're kind. And lovely."

"Thank you."

The lady turned her attention back to Rafe. "Come by the house sometime. I promise to put that other business behind us."

Shannon detected a hint of a plea in the words.

"I'll do that, Mother. Give my love to the girls."

His mother moved on, greeting more people, chatting with several, and then sent a lingering look over her shoulder at Rafe.

"Your mother's very gracious."

"She is. She did her best by me and my sisters after our father died. I'm afraid I'm a disappointment to her."

"You don't really believe that, do you? I saw the pride in her eyes when she looked at you. She loves you. Maybe she just doesn't know how to say it."

"I know she loves me. I just wish she could see that I made the right choice for me." If there'd been a plea in the mother's voice, there was wistfulness in the son's.

Shannon's heart ached for them. She wanted to tell Rafe and his mother to be grateful that they had the other in their lives at all. Old hurt bloomed, feelings of bewilderment and abandonment emerging as fresh as the days that her mother, then her father, had left.

It had been years since she'd seen either of her parents. They'd made it plain that they had their own lives. She was an inconvenience, a reminder of past troubles. The last she'd heard they were happy with their new families. She was glad for them; at the same time, she doubted they had a place in their lives for her, except for the occasional Christmas or birthday card.

It was something to ponder later. Not now. Her head was buzzing, first with her boss's warning then with Calhoun's hint that she might be the next DA. Did one have something to do with the other? She didn't see how, but little was making sense tonight. Including her feelings for Rafe.

Needing a moment to collect her thoughts, she turned to him. "I'm going to freshen up."

He followed her to the rear of the ballroom, where the restrooms were located.

Inside the luxurious restroom, a woman brushed by her. A sting on her arm caused Shannon to pause. It was nothing, barely a pinprick, but a wave of dizziness overtook her.

The same woman, a scarf draped around her throat and partially covering her face, came to her aid. "Can I help you?"

"No... I don't—" The words caught in her throat, and she swayed. What was going on? She'd been fine only seconds ago, and now she could barely stand. Goose bumps peppered her arms, yet heat caressed her body. She tried to make her way to one of the velvet-covered stools in front of a long marble counter.

"You'll be all right." The woman put an arm around Shannon's waist and started to lead her out of the restroom. "Come with me. I'll take you somewhere you can lie down. Everything will be fine. You'll see."

Shannon knew she should resist, but she was powerless to do so. It was as if an invisible force compelled her to do as the woman instructed. As the two of them exited the restroom, Rafe came running in their direction.

"Shannon!"

At that moment, two men sprang forward.

SIX

Rafe didn't retreat, as the men no doubt expected, but moved in and slammed his elbow into one's gut and kicked out with his right leg, catching the other in the kidney. Both men grunted, clutched their injured areas and looked at each other in consternation.

Guests were scattering, their screams ripping through the air. Rafe paid no attention as the first man drew a knife from a sheath at his ankle and came at him with murder in his eyes.

Rafe grabbed the man's wrist, then twisted back and up, forcing him to drop the knife. His face twisted in a grimace of pain, probably from the blow to his kidneys. The second man made a half-hearted rush toward Rafe. He stepped sideways, then grabbed the man by the shoulder, spun him around and head-butted him. He dropped to the floor with scarcely a moan.

The first one hightailed it to the stairs. Instinct had Rafe itching to go after him, but protecting Shannon came first. When he turned to see the woman who had appeared from the restroom with Shannon, her shoulder was beneath Shannon's arm, and she was making her way to the bank of elevators. He took off after them.

When she saw that one of her partners was out of commission and the other had taken off, she released Shannon and ran.

Rafe caught Shannon just before she slumped to the floor. He carried her to a sofa, punched in 911 on his phone and gave the location, then called S&J.

He stared down at her, his breath halting as he took in the alarming paleness of her face. The vitality that was so much a part of her was missing. She needed warmth, so he shrugged off his tuxedo jacket and spread it over her. It was so big that it nearly swallowed her whole.

With gratitude, he handed her over to the EMTs when they arrived. When they took her to the ambulance, Rafe climbed in with them. One look at his expression and the weapon holstered at his shoulder and they didn't offer any objections when he announced he was going with them.

The trip to the hospital was a blur of sirens and lights, but his attention was all on Shannon. When her hand slipped off the gurney, he reached for it and pressed it between his own, ignoring the glare the EMT sent his way.

At the hospital, Shannon was whisked away. He paced the length of the hallway outside the emergency room, berating himself. How had it happened? She'd been away from him for less than a minute.

He pushed all of the questions from his mind and focused on Shannon. Nothing else mattered.

When a doctor appeared, Rafe nearly jumped on him. "What is it, doctor?"

Rafe had already shown his bona fides as a bodyguard and explained the situation to the doctor.

"We did a blood test. It's as we thought. She's been drugged. Scopolamine."

"I know what scopolamine does." Rafe slammed his fist into his open palm, impatience shimmering through him. It terrified him what might have happened to Shannon. A drug like that made anyone defenseless and unable to resist suggestions or commands.

"When can I see her?"

"Not for another hour. Why don't you go home and get some rest? Now, if you'll excuse me." With that, the doctor moved on.

While Rafe appreciated the concern, he wouldn't be leaving Shannon. After calling S&J and filling them in on this development, Rafe paced the corridor.

At last, he was finally allowed in the room.

Shannon looked small and vulnerable in the hospital bed, a stark contrast to her normal energy and determination. He wanted to scoop her up and carry her away from all the ugliness that had come raining down on her.

Machines monitored her breathing and blood pressure.

Rafe pulled up a chair as close to the bed as possible and watched her, simply watched her. "Lord, please watch over Shannon. I know Your love is infinite."

The steady blip of the machines lulled him into a drowsy state. He braced his elbows on the side of the mattress and rested his head in the cradle of his hands. When his eyelids grew heavy, he let them drift closed and the day wash out of him. Tension rolled through and out, and he gave himself up to sleep. It was a fitful sleep with images of Shannon being dragged away by unseen enemies.

How long he slept, he couldn't have said, but when he woke, it was to find Shannon smiling at him. Her face was pale and drawn, but she looked alert, and the blankness in her earlier expression was absent.

"You're here. I knew you would be." With the hand not tethered to tubes, she reached for his. "Thank you."

Her words humbled him. "I don't deserve that.

I let them get to you." For that, he doubted he could forgive himself.

"No, you saved me. I don't know what the woman would have done if you hadn't come along when you did."

"She should never have gotten that close." His voice turned husky as he thought about what might have happened. It had been close. Too close. Guilt that he'd failed to protect her overtook him and turned his voice gruff.

"Enough of that. You saved me. That's all that matters."

He was responsible.

It was fine to blame Newton and his crew for what had happened, but Rafe had accepted the job of keeping Shannon safe and he'd failed. During the night, the knowledge had settled over him like an Afghanistan sandstorm, rasping away at his nerve endings, leaving his emotions raw and bleeding. He'd survived more than one sandstorm, but he didn't know if he'd survive this one.

Upon being released from the hospital, Shannon refused to spend the day at home resting, as the doctor had suggested. After a trip home to shower and change clothes, she and Rafe made yet another trip to the police station to give a statement.

When she arrived at work, she shook her head

to questions from her coworkers, told everyone she was all right and shut herself in her office.

Rafe didn't hover. But he came close.

She'd done her best to assure him that she was okay, but he continued to blame himself. When she excused herself to go to the restroom and he followed her, she'd had enough.

Head up, chin thrust forward, she fisted her hands on her hips. "You're my bodyguard. Not my nursemaid. Last night happened. Thanks to you, I'm fine. Get over it."

He cupped her shoulders. "You could have been killed." His voice rose with every syllable. "Do you understand that? *You could have been killed.* What if I hadn't gotten to you in time?"

"But you did."

"Yeah. This time. But what about the next? And the one after that?"

"I don't know," she said honestly. "But what I do know is that I trust you. That should be enough for you. So stop blaming yourself or—" she assumed a fierce expression "—I'll have to get rough with you."

He held up his hands in a gesture of surrender, though his brow was creased with concern. "Okay. I'll stop hovering."

She asked her assistant, Georgia, to hold her calls and, for the rest of the day, worked without disruption...until Georgia burst into the office.

Shannon looked up in annoyance. "I thought I told you—"

"Ms. DeFord, it's Mrs. Kimball," the secretary announced, her urgent voice at odds with her normally easygoing manner.

For Georgia to interrupt meant something had happened. Something bad. "What about her?"

"She's in the hospital. Word is that she was beaten pretty badly. I can try to find out more, but—"

Shannon's back snapped ramrod-straight as she listened. When Georgia finished, Shannon didn't bother asking for more details. She'd find out soon enough. She had only one question now. "Which hospital?"

"County."

Shannon looked at Rafe. "We've got to get to County Hospital. Now."

Rafe made the trip in record time. They found Mrs. Kimball's room, only to be told that she couldn't receive visitors.

Shannon peered through the glass window of the door and saw her witness swathed in bandages, her right arm in a cast and left leg in a sling contraption to keep it elevated.

When a doctor approached, Shannon pulled out her ID as a DDA. "What can you tell me about her condition?"

"She's in a medically induced coma. From the

indentations on her skull, face and body, somebody beat her with a tire iron." The doctor's voice hardened. "Whoever did this wanted to make sure she wasn't going anywhere for a long time. It's a wonder she's still alive. As it is, we don't know if she'll be able to walk or talk or even breathe on her own after we wake her up."

Tears stung Shannon's eyes. What had she done by encouraging Mrs. Kimball to testify?

A young man moved in her direction and would have gotten in her face if Rafe hadn't pushed himself between Shannon and him.

Gently, she motioned Rafe aside so that she faced Daniel Kimball. So furious was Mrs. Kimball's son that the whites of his eyes showed all around the irises.

"You're to blame for this," he accused. "You badgered my mother into agreeing to testify, wouldn't let up until she said yes. I hope you're happy."

Shannon had met Mrs. Kimball's son before and hadn't been impressed. He had treated his mother with an impatient air, frequently interrupting her if she took too long to tell her story.

Where Mrs. Kimball was determined to do the right thing, her son wanted to know what was in it for them if she testified and had actually asked if there was a reward for doing so.

None of that mattered now.

Shannon heard the fear behind the words, fear that his mother might never regain consciousness. That tempered her previous annoyance with him. "Mr. Kimball, I'm so sorry. And I'm far from happy."

"Is that all you have to say? You're sorry?" Anger vibrated in Daniel's voice. Anger and something else. Something that wasn't pretty.

She held her ground. Once again, Rafe made to step forward, but Shannon held him back. "Mr. Kimball, I understand that you're upset, but—"

"Don't. Just don't. Keep your sympathy to yourself. If not for you, my mother wouldn't be in the hospital, all banged up.

"It's your fault," he said, continuing with his tirade. "You were the one who pushed her to testify against those animals. You nearly ordered her to do so, saying that it was her civic duty. Where did her civic duty get her? You heard the doctor say it's a wonder that she's still alive. They broke three bones and beat her in the face so badly that she'll need extensive plastic surgery if she survives at all."

"I'm sorry. More sorry than I can say." Shannon reached out to touch Daniel's arm, but he jerked away.

"You asked too much from her. She can't breathe on her own, can't even talk." His words were bitter, his face even more so.

Beneath the anger, though, was genuine grief. In the end, he was only a son worried over his mother, causing Shannon's heart to soften.

She understood that, and it tempered her response. "You have every right to be angry. At the men who did this. And at me."

That appeared to take him aback. He was a handsome man, but there was a weakness in him that emphasized there was little of his mother in him.

"After my father died, all my mother ever wanted was to take care of herself and me," he said, the tears in his eyes revealing that grief was overcoming his anger. "She saved for years to buy her store. What did it get her but this?" He pointed through the glass door to where his mother was lying like a broken doll in a hospital bed. "Why did they have to hurt her that way?"

Shannon had no answer to that and turned back to look at Mrs. Kimball once more. She was a small woman who looked even tinier hooked up to tubes and monitors.

"If there is any justice, the men she was going to testify against would be in the hospital. Not her."

Shannon couldn't help sharing his sentiment. Still, she couldn't condone vigilantism. "We have no proof that Newton and his men did this," she pointed out before wincing at the prim words.

Daniel snorted.

She could hardly blame him. She knew, just as he did, that Newton had ordered his men to beat up his mother.

"I'm sorry," she repeated. She didn't bother saying what she was sorry for. There was too much she regretted. An engulfing wave of guilt swamped her, along with a bone-deep grief.

Rafe took her arm and started down the corridor. "C'mon. Let's get you out of here."

"I hope you sleep well tonight, Ms. Deputy District Attorney," Daniel called after her. "I hope you get what you deserve for allowing this to happen."

Rafe didn't say anything more until they were outside. "He had no right coming down on you that way."

Her shoulders slumped in defeat and sorrow. "He was right. I am to blame that his mother is in the hospital."

Rafe wrapped an arm around her shoulders. "That's garbage and you know it. The blame belongs to Newton and his crew. This is *not* on you. You're not as smart as I think you are if you spend one minute beating yourself up over it."

"But I persuaded Mrs. Kimball to testify. She came forward, and I was so happy to have a witness that I didn't think about what could happen to her. What *did* happen."

"She decided to testify because it was the right thing to do." Rafe's mouth stretched into a hard line. "I'm with her son on one thing, though. I'd like to have five minutes alone with Newton. It might be interesting to see how he fared against someone who could fight back."

The wolf came into his eyes. The warrior. The hunter. And she shivered at what she read there.

She didn't bother trying to dissuade Rafe on the point as she had Daniel because she felt the same. Determination had her setting her shoulders. As horrible as what had been done to Mrs. Kimball, she wouldn't let it deter her from doing her job. She couldn't allow it to cause her to unravel. "All the more reason to bring them to justice. The right way." Without Mrs. Kimball's testimony, though, Shannon didn't have much of a case.

"You're too smart not to know that they've burned their bridges with this. There's no going back. Before, it was just property damage, extortion and some minor rough stuff. Anything goes now, including attempted murder. You're still in their way. They won't hesitate to take you out."

"If you're trying to scare me, you've succeeded." She'd meant the words to come off as light. Instead, they trembled with fear.

"You're right—I am trying to scare you. I want you to know what you're up against."

It shamed her to admit, even to herself, that she'd considered backing away from the case, but if she ran from this, how could she trust herself not to run the next time things turned dangerous? She had to see this through. Not just for Mrs. Kimball and the other shop owners, but for herself.

She refused to do less. To be less.

"I mean to win this case and when I do, it will send a message—no one has the right to intimidate others."

Rafe nodded slowly. "That's a powerful message."

"It's meant to be."

She wasn't her father. She didn't run at the first sign of trouble. She didn't run. Period.

SEVEN

After stopping to pick up something to eat, Rafe and Shannon headed back to her office, taking the food with them. He knew she needed time to decompress, so he took a scenic drive through the foothills that served as the gatekeepers to the rugged Rockies. Blankets of flowers turned the hills blue.

Though he knew there was little possibility of convincing her to hand over the case to someone else, he had to try. Protecting her came first. If he had to, he'd take down Newton and his men himself.

Delta style.

By the time they reached the city, Shannon seemed less stressed, and he knew that going the longer route had been worth the extra time.

While she sat at her desk to eat one of the burgers they'd ordered, he leaned against a wall and folded his arms over his chest. The pose was laid-back; the tension roiling through him was not. "The attack on Mrs. Kimball puts a new spin on things."

She nodded tersely. "More than ever, I have to stop Newton and his gang."

"Maybe it's time to do what your boss suggested."

"You mean give up?"

He chose his next words with care. "I mean take a step back. After what you've been through, no one would blame you. You could still keep your hand in, but you don't have to be point person on the case."

Shannon tilted her head, her gaze inquisitive. "If it were you, would you back down?"

"That's different."

Disappointment flooded her eyes, and he wanted to yank back his words and stuff them down his throat. "Because you're a man?"

No sense in trying to pull his foot out of his mouth. The damage was done. Still, he tried. "Because I can take care of myself." That was neutral, wasn't it?

"And I can't? Don't forget, I was there with you in the woods when those men came after us."

"That's right," he agreed. "You were. And you did a great job, but you're going up against men who could and would kill you with nothing more than a twist of their hands and with no more thought than they'd give to squashing a bug.

"These aren't your average street punks. They're trained, maybe paramilitary, and know how to inflict maximum pain without breaking a sweat."

"When you were in Afghanistan and were ordered to take down enemy troops, did you back off because it was dangerous?"

"No, but that was—"

"Don't you dare say it was different," she warned. "It's exactly the same."

Rafe made a grumbling noise. "You're playing with fire."

She stood and folded her arms across her chest. "I'm not backing down."

"Why are you so hardheaded?"

"You mean, why am I just like you?"

His mouth canted at one corner at her swift comeback. "Yeah, I guess that's what I mean. Like I said, no one would blame you for stepping back on this. Including me."

"*I'd* blame me. I promised myself that I would never run. I have to stand up to those who want to destroy our city, and I have to stand up for myself. I couldn't live with myself if I turned my back on this." She looked down at her hands, then lifted her gaze to his.

Shadows borne of fatigue and worry had taken up residence beneath her eyes, but they only underscored her determination to fight for justice.

She didn't let up, even when she was exhausted. He saw the weariness breaking through in her face, pulling at her, but never once had she hinted that she needed to rest.

It was only one of the reasons he liked her as he did.

Rafe considered the brutal acts that Newton and his crew had committed. They operated as though they were untouchable. Or coated with Teflon. Maybe that Teflon would lead them to the people behind the attacks.

"I appreciate you caring about what happens to me, but I have to do this. Whatever the risks. I'm not backing down. If you can't handle that, I'll go it alone."

He hadn't expected anything else. "I'm not leaving."

"Why not?"

"Because I believe in what you're doing."

A startled expression filled her eyes. "You do?"

"I do."

"Then why were you trying to get me to quit the case?" There was hurt in her voice—hurt and bewilderment.

"I wanted you to realize what you're going up against. Newton and whoever is behind him don't play by the same rules you and I do. I don't want to see you harmed." He paused and then added, "Or worse." He was walking a fine line between protecting Shannon and keeping himself from becoming involved with her.

Mentally he scoffed at that. Who was he trying to fool? He already had feelings for her, despite warning himself of the danger of becoming involved with a woman, especially one as beautiful as Shannon. His fiancée had cheated on him while he'd been deployed, and though he'd told himself that not every woman cheated, the lesson had been seared into his mind and his heart.

"I get it," she said, but he could tell that she didn't fully understand.

"Cruelty is a way of life for some people." He scrubbed his hands over his face in a futile attempt to wipe away memories.

"I suppose you've seen a lot," she said.

"Too much."

"During your time in Afghanistan?" Her voice was tentative, as though she didn't want to stir up bad memories.

"Yeah." He left it at that. He didn't share his time in Afghanistan. Not with anyone. What he'd seen and done there had forever changed him.

Shannon looked at him. When he didn't say anything, she skimmed her fingers down his arm. "I'm sorry."

"For what?"

"For whatever put the sadness in your eyes."

"I'm okay." Without making too much of it, he

shook off her hand. He wasn't in the mood for sympathy. Not from Shannon. Not from anyone. Ever since he'd lost his leg, he'd shunned any attempt on the part of others to offer sympathy. He could live with losing part of his leg; what he couldn't live with was pity.

"Are you?"

He was grateful when she didn't follow up with more questions.

Protecting Shannon meant he was all in. That was the only way he knew how to do his job, be it in Afghanistan or here.

"I know what the justice system is up against," she said. "The cops—most of them, anyway— do their best to round up the bad guys. People like me do their best to prosecute them. And the judges do their best to sentence them fairly and justly. If we do our jobs well, we may stay one step ahead of the crooks, but there are always more coming, with new ways to cheat the system. Sometimes we fall behind, so we double our efforts just to catch up."

"Why do you do it?" He honestly wanted to know.

"Because I want to make a difference. Like you."

He'd felt that way at one time, but he had seen too many children starving, too many young boys pressed into fighting for an unjust cause, too many wives and mothers weeping at the loss of husbands and sons, to believe he could make a real difference in the world. In the end, all he could do was to pray for them.

Shannon reflected on Rafe's warning. He hadn't pulled his punches. Not that she'd expected he would.

Despite her annoyance with him in wanting her to step away, he was one of the good guys.

Rafe wore his integrity and honor quietly, but it shone through in everything he did. His belief in the Lord had sustained him through what had to be one of the most horrific experiences anyone could endure. It had not turned him bitter. Rather, it had honed his compassion for others.

Her faith had once been a wellspring of strength for her, too, and she'd naively believed that nothing could shake it. How wrong she'd been.

Envy took root in her heart. Could she find that for herself? The years stretched long and empty before her as she thought of dealing with life without the Lord on her side.

Had she made a monumental mistake in turning away from Him? She'd taken His silence when she'd begged for answers to mean He didn't care. Could she learn to trust Him, as Rafe did? Despite what he'd been through, Rafe remained steadfast in his faith.

Perhaps He had answered her after all in His own way, a way she was too blind to see and too stubborn to appreciate. Could she welcome Him into her life once more?

The answers she sought continued to elude her, though, and she knew that she couldn't untangle her feelings about the Lord when the case pressed on her from all sides.

Right now she had to convince Rafe that she could handle this case and all that went with it. "I'll be all right, because I know you'll be there to keep me safe."

He smiled crookedly. "You put too much faith in me."

"You're the believer. What should I do?"

"Put your faith in God," he answered so promptly that she knew the answer was borne of long belief. "The Lord is the One Who holds the power. The only One."

"Are you saying I shouldn't have faith in you?"

There was that crooked smile again, one that made her want to place her thumbs at the corners of it and turn it into a full smile. What would his reaction be if she did such a thing?

She pushed aside that thought and listened as Rafe explained.

"I'm saying you should put your faith in the One who loved us enough to die for us. If I have any skill, it's because the Lord has given it to me. People will let you down, but He never will."

"Who let you down?" she said, daring to ask. It was none of her business, but she wanted to know who had caused him so much pain.

"It's not a particularly interesting story."

"I don't need interesting stories. Just the truth." With that, she realized that she wanted to know more about Rafe, to understand the man as well as the bodyguard.

She wasn't getting emotionally involved with him, she assured herself. It was only prudent, after all, to know who was protecting her.

"When I returned from Afghanistan, I spent the next year in and out of hospitals and rehab. I was engaged at the time and told my fiancée not to come see me until I was up and walking under my own steam. It didn't take much to convince her. Three months later, I told her I was ready for a visit.

"Victoria happened to show up when a therapist was fitting me with a prosthetic leg. I'll never forget the horror on her face. She did her best to cover it up, but it was enough. A day later, a package was delivered to me. I found the engagement ring I'd given her inside along with a note saying that she couldn't handle my leg." He lifted a shoulder in a what-are-you-going-to-do-about-it? shrug.

Shannon regarded him curiously. He sounded like there was more to the story, something more important, something that went far deeper than his fiancée's feelings about his leg, and though she wanted to ask what he wasn't telling her, she held her tongue. If Rafe didn't want to share, she had to respect that.

Maybe someday.

She knew Rafe wouldn't want sympathy, might even throw it back in her face. Instead, she said, "That was her great loss."

"My mother said the same thing."

Shannon thought of the gracious and intelligent woman she'd met at the fundraiser. "Your mother's a smart lady."

"Yeah. She is."

"What happened to your fiancée?"

"I heard that she married a doctor, lives in Cherry Creek and drives a Bentley. She got what she wanted."

"You're better off without her." Without even knowing the woman, Shannon understood that Rafe's ex-fiancée was selfish, shallow and totally lacking in values if she turned away a good man like him.

Once more, that crooked smile came out. "Once I got over it, I realized she'd done me a favor. We'd have been miserable together. She wanted something different. Turns out, so did I."

His gaze was warm as it rested on her, and she resisted the urge to squirm. She wasn't accustomed to such attention and, quite frankly, she didn't know what to do with it. Frantically, she searched for what they'd been talking about before she'd derailed the conversation; her mind, though, went blank of everything but the man at her side.

Rafe was here to keep her safe, nothing more, but her heart was having a hard time accepting that. A very hard time.

EIGHT

Why had he told Shannon so much about one of the most painful periods of his life? Rafe wondered. He rarely spoke of his ex-fiancée—in fact, he had actively discouraged personal questions from his friends at S&J. But with Shannon, he'd felt compelled to tell her what had happened and not to gloss over the ugly parts.

And felt better for it.

As open as he'd been, however, he hadn't shared everything about that time of his life. His ex-fiancée had betrayed him in a far worse way than simply being repelled by his prosthetic leg. When she'd confessed to cheating on him, he knew it was truly over. Love could survive a lot of things, but a lack of trust was not one of them.

It was time to leave that part of his life where it belonged. In the past. He had a job to do.

"Newton and his crew have to have someone big protecting them," he said. "Someone with a lot of pull in the city. And a lot of money. That makes them even more dangerous."

"If you're going to suggest that I back down again—"

"No. I know you're in for the long haul. I'm just trying to figure out who's backing Newton. And why."

The question hummed between them.

Shannon pointed to the map she had tacked to the wall. "I've asked myself over and over, why Newton and his men went after this block of shops. It's not like any of them make a lot of money. Certainly not enough to pay much in protection money.

"There's a dry cleaner, tailor, a mom-and-pop grocery store, a diner, a pawn shop and a jewelry-repair place. Why not go after this section?" She moved her finger to indicate a block in an upscale part of the area, where businesses like boutique coffee shops and trendy restaurants catered to wealthy professionals and up-and-coming millennials.

Rafe perched on the edge of the desk. "That's a good question. What did you come up with?"

"Nothing. That's the problem." She continued staring at the map as though the sheer act of doing so would provide the answer they needed.

"Do the storekeepers own the property or lease it?" he asked.

"Own." She dragged a hand through her hair, lifting it off her neck then letting it fall free once more. "What makes them so special? All of them have been there for at least a decade, some much longer."

"Maybe it's not the shops themselves but the land they sit on that's so valuable."

Shannon whirled around "I think you're on to something."

"Yeah?"

"Yeah." She spun back to study the map once more. "Look at where this block is located. It's the hub of the entire area. What if something major is in the works? Something that's going to make that property skyrocket?"

"Like what?"

"I don't know."

That was the problem. There was too much they didn't know. He felt like he was shadow-boxing in the dark.

He stared out the window at the Denver cityscape, just a few miles to the south, but he wasn't seeing the cityscape at all. Rather, a puzzle with a key piece missing faced him. "Did you read the story of Odysseus?"

Shannon's eyes widened, but she nodded. "It's been a while, but yes."

"Then you'll remember that he returned home after twenty years. During those years, his wife was pursued by numerous suitors. Odysseus wanted to see them for himself, so he disguised himself as a beggar. No one recognized him except for his dog, Argos. Argos had been put out on the dung heap and left to die, but he recognized his master. He barked then died."

"I know the story," she reminded him.

"Do you remember why Argos recognized Odysseus?" He didn't wait for her answer. "He looked past the noise and saw the truth. The rest of it—the sores, the fleas, the filth—was just noise, not pertinent. I think that's what we're doing, falling victim to noise. It's a smoke screen, so that we don't see what's really going on. We have to be like Argos and see the truth. Or smell it."

She wrinkled her nose. "How do we know what the truth is?"

"We start by figuring out who stands to gain if those stores are sold, either as a block or one by one. Grab your stuff. We have some digging to do."

She grabbed her briefcase and slid her laptop inside. "Where're we heading?"

"Hall of records."

The hall of records would contain information not only about the various properties involved, but also about those surrounding the targeted block. The purchase price of the properties. Date of transactions. Name of buyers.

Rafe took the briefcase from her. "What do you have in here? Rocks?"

"My laptop. Books. Files. And yesterday's lunch that I forgot to eat."

"No wonder you're so skinny."

"I prefer to think of it as fashionably slender."

Rafe was smiling, but the smile slipped as he thought of what Shannon had taken on. Newton and his men weren't going away. Well, neither was he.

The trip to the hall of records didn't give them much that they didn't already know.

Shannon said as much on their way back to the office. "A wasted trip."

Rafe's forehead creased in a frown. "Maybe we're not asking the right questions."

"What questions should we be asking?"

"I don't know."

Although Rafe didn't crowd her as she worked through the rest of the day, his question remained on the top of her mind as she tried to balance the load between her other cases and what she had begun to think of as the Kimball case. Mrs. Kimball deserved justice, and Shannon was determined to get it for her.

At 7:00 p.m., Shannon was still working and

showed no signs of stopping. She was cross-eyed and hungry, but though her body was screaming with exhaustion, her mind was truly weary from wading through reams of paper.

If she could work through the night, there was a slim possibility that she might catch up. Almost. By 9:00 p.m., though, she accepted that she needed food and sleep.

Rafe crossed the room to her desk. "Time's up."

Though she'd just told herself the same thing, she felt bound to protest, thinking of the work she still had to do. "I just have to finish up a brief."

"There's nothing that can't wait until morning."

"How do you—?"

"You're exhausted. We're going to pick up a pizza and take it back to your place."

Her stomach growled as though on cue. She blushed and Rafe grinned at the telltale sign that she was hungry. She closed down her computer and picked up her purse. "Let's go."

In the parking lot, two shadows moved in their direction.

Rafe handed Shannon his keys. "Go to the car and get out of here. Don't stop until you reach a police station."

"No."

"We don't have time to argue." He gave her a gentle push in the direction of the car.

She felt more than heard the men advancing and turned slowly.

"Is there a problem?" Rafe asked.

"You could say that," the taller of the two men said. "Our boss doesn't like what your girlfriend's been saying."

Rafe didn't bother correcting the man about his and Shannon's relationship. "The lady only tells the truth. If your boss doesn't like the truth, that's his problem."

"Yeah? Well, my boss has other ideas." He snapped his attention to Shannon. "Lady, listen up and listen good. Take a trip and maybe you'll live to see another day. Stay, and you'll live to regret it." He let out a menacing laugh. "Or maybe you won't. Live, that is. Makes no difference to me."

The men wanted to play with them, much like a cat might play with a mouse before pouncing and killing it. The cold cast to their eyes told her that they would enjoy the game, but that they would kill her and Rafe when the time came.

She had her answer when she realized that gunshots would draw unwanted attention.

Despite the man's assertion that Shannon could "take a trip," she knew that she and Rafe weren't meant to walk away from this. She stepped out from behind him. "Maybe your boss better re-think things. Because I'm not going anywhere." She planted her hands on her hips and stared him down.

Rafe pulled her behind him once more and squared off with the big man. "Get out of here," he told Shannon. "I'll take care of these two."

"I'll leave when you do."

"You could out-stubborn a mule," he muttered.

He'd barely finished the last word before the first man came at him, fists raised. Though Rafe was not small by any means, the attacker topped him by at least two inches and probably thirty pounds, but it wasn't his size that intimidated her. It was the coldness in his eyes, which that prom-ised he'd make anyone who went up against him wish they hadn't. He wouldn't go down easily. If he went down at all.

"Go," Rafe ordered Shannon once more.

But she didn't hightail to the car as he'd or-dered. Instead she stepped up to confront the sec-ond man as she heard the first one throw a taunt at Rafe.

"You're gonna hurt before I take you out. I'm gonna make sure of it."

No way was she going to leave Rafe to face the two men on his own. The goons were a cli-ché of muscle-bound hired help, but just because they were bulked up didn't mean they weren't intelligent.

On the contrary, cunning intelligence gleamed in the man's eyes as she faced him. It told her that he knew what she was thinking and was amused by it.

Amusement was the last thing she was feeling.

"You can make this hard on yourself or you can make it easy. Either way's the same to me." More alarming than a voice edgy with menace was one of total indifference.

"You're going to kill me either way," she said.

"Yeah, but there's hard and there's easy. You'd be smart to choose easy."

His face was a slab of granite that appeared to be taken straight from a mountainside. A jutting chin and a nose that looked like it had been broken more than once completed the picture. Meanness burnished the space between his eyebrows.

Taking her out was a job, no more, no less. A business transaction that he would carry out with a minimum of fuss.

With a barrel chest and long arms ropy with muscle and sinew, he came at her swinging fists the size of Virginia hams. She angled away from him, but there was no way she could escape his reach forever.

After ducking beneath the first punch, she watched him bounce away on the balls of his feet and had the lowering feeling that he had never intended to hit her with that initial punch, that he had let her get away unscathed just to mess with her.

That stiffened her backbone and her resolve.

He swept out a leg and kicked her in the gut. Excruciating pain radiated through her, and every fiber of her body screamed in silent agony. She had the presence of mind to windmill her arms in an attempt to stay on her feet, but she was close, too close, to toppling over. If she did that, she feared she was finished.

Shannon sucked in a large gulp of air. She'd need every bit of it if she was going to come out on top in a fight with him. Much as she prided herself on being able to take care of herself, she was no match for the man who loomed over her.

She didn't back up. Nor did she look away. She held her ground and his gaze, refusing to flinch at the flat expression in his eyes.

"You look mighty tiny to be trading punches with me, lil lady." The exaggerated accent did nothing to change her mind about the man's shrewdness. He was toying with her, telling her that she couldn't possibly best him in a fight.

He glanced over at his partner, saw him pounding on Rafe. And smiled.

Find the weak spot and use it. Her brother's words echoed in her mind as she made her move.

She kicked out a leg and hooked it behind his knee. He teetered slightly but remained on his feet with minimal effort. With the benefit of surprise, she moved in close and rained blows on his midsection, wincing at the feebleness of them against his rock-hard abs.

"Surprised me there, you did," he said, favoring her with a look of grudging respect and then hissing through his teeth. "Let's dance again."

"Yeah. Let's dance."

The dark granite of his face deepened a notch at her comeback. He wouldn't be so easy to surprise the next time. When he moved in on her, she struck out with her right fist, the blow connecting with his chin.

He took a moment to rub at his chin, his hand coming away with blood where she'd split the skin. "You made a big mistake there," he said. "Yes, sirree, a mighty big mistake. Making me mad is the last thing you want to do." A load of menace punctuated each word.

He was wrong there.

The last thing she wanted to do was to let him get his hands on her. Thanks to Jeff, she had some Krav Maga, which was a type of martial arts practiced by Israeli special forces, but she wasn't a professionally trained fighter, and her man had more than a hundred pounds on her.

Though he was big, he wasn't fat. Instead, he appeared to be all muscle.

During her calculations, he'd moved closer. Too close. When he clapped her head between his palms, her ears were ringing. She'd never known what the phrase meant until that moment when a clanging noise jangled through her head. It was a wonder she could hear at all.

A self-satisfied sneer stretched across his mouth.

She realized she was breathing through her mouth, a giveaway that she was terrified. She shivered at the confidence in his eyes, a confidence that said he planned to wipe the floor with her. She came in low and gave him a short jab in the gut. The blow was minor, but it was enough to have his eyes narrowing.

Following up on that small victory, she shifted, putting more weight on her left leg, while getting ready to strike with her right.

"C'mon, big man," she taunted. "You're not going to let a woman best you, are you?"

Ego and temper were a bad combination. She figured a man like him had his share of both. And she'd use both against him.

He huffed out a sound of impatience tinged with anger and got in a blow to her jaw, sending her sprawling to the ground. Then he reared back and kicked her in the side. The air whooshed from her lungs in a shockingly painful gust. She scrabbled backward on her hands, but she wasn't quick enough to save herself from another bruising kick to the ribs.

When he threw himself at her, she twisted away, causing him to miss her by scant inches. She grabbed for whatever she could reach and came away with a clod of mud, probably left by a tire. With all the force she could summon, she threw it in his face.

He spit out mud and glowered at her, the daggers in his gaze promising he'd make her regret that particular move.

She managed to put a little distance between them while he swiped a hand over his face. But now she was winded, her ribs aching, and she knew she was done for if she didn't do something quickly. A recent storm had downed some tree branches. Looking wildly about, she spied a branch that was the size of a bat. She made a swipe for it, grazing it with her fingertips. One more try, and she closed her fingers around it.

She stood and swung for all she was worth. The makeshift weapon caught him in the lower side. Had she hit him in the kidney?

Again.

Deliberately hurting someone wasn't in her wheelhouse, but she wasn't about to let him get his hands on her. He wasn't there to issue a warning. No, his job was to make her hurt and kill her. Along with Rafe.

A grunt from her bodyguard had her glancing in his direction. He hadn't signed on to get beaten by a giant.

That thought temporarily knocked her off her game, and her foe got in another swipe to her jaw. Pain sang through her neck, jaw and face. She bared her teeth and let loose with a kick to his solar plexus. It scarcely fazed him, but at least she'd shown him that he couldn't come at her without some kind of response.

He flexed his arms and clenched his hands into supersized fists. If one of those fists connected with her again, she would be out flat. She knew it from his gaze, one that was hot with the kind of fury that told her she'd succeeded in making him angry and she was now going to pay for it.

Before she realized what was happening, he picked her up by the shoulders and held her dangling in the air, her feet uselessly kicking. He held her there for long seconds before dropping her to the ground. She groaned and tried to stand. The first try was a bust, and she tried again. When she regained her feet, he was grinning at her.

A mistake on his part. He should have finished her off when he'd had the opportunity, but he was enjoying gloating too much.

And then she saw it. He rubbed at his shoulder and scowled. Had the blow he'd given her earlier jarred something loose in his shoulder? Whatever the cause, it was vulnerable, and she intended to exploit it.

When he advanced, she spun and delivered a hard jab to his shoulder.

Agony flared in his eyes and told her that she'd been right. His shoulder was a weak spot. Maybe it had sustained some kind of earlier injury. The suffering she read in his eyes couldn't be caused by the punch she'd given him. She repeated the move before he had time to retaliate.

This time, he gave a mighty groan. His knees buckled, but he remained standing. What would it take to put him down? He straightened his legs and shot a look of pure viciousness at her. He put a considerable amount of his weight on his back foot and lined up a straight dive for her.

If he got his hands on her again, she'd be a goner. She shifted her hips, then pushed off on the right foot, arms raised, and shoulders squared. It was an offensive position, one Jeff had taught her.

When the man charged her, she kicked out, catching his knee in the side, where it was most vulnerable. She smashed her heel into it with every ounce of strength she possessed.

The man had more than two hundred and fifty pounds bearing down on his knee and a hundred and twenty driving straight through it. In that instant of impact, the bone splintered, and his leg folded back in the wrong direction.

Letting out an inhuman noise, he went down hard, landing on his head, even with his arms outstretched to break the fall. His left temple bounced on the unforgiving surface. The ground seemed to shudder beneath him. For a full ten seconds, he didn't utter a single sound. And then his shattered kneecap caused him to writhe and moan in pain.

When Rafe's opponent came at him a second time, he blocked the first blow, but he had some serious moves and used them with a proficiency that had Rafe thinking he'd probably been in the military or had worked as a mercenary. His opponent led with his right and managed to get in a blow to Rafe's jaw. Pain exploded through his head.

Rafe shook it off and pulled back, just enough to give himself room to maneuver and get in a hard jab to the man's side. A rhythm developed, one Rafe had always thought of in terms of fencing: feint, parry, thrust. Only the moves were made with feet and fists rather than foils.

The two men were evenly matched, and Rafe knew he was going to have to use every bit of skill he had to come out on top. He watched his man's moves and noted that he touched his nose

before he advanced, an unconscious tell that tele-
graphed his intentions.

When his adversary slammed a fist to the side
of Rafe's head, he knew he was in trouble. A deep
maroon fringed his eyesight. Double vision and
a wave of dizziness left him reeling. Reeling and
vulnerable.

His best opportunity for survival was to use
the man's momentum against him. "Come on,"
he taunted. "Let's see if you've got any more."

Eyes cold and flat as a snake's, the big man
advanced. "You wanna see what I've got? Come
on. I'll give you a·taste if you're man enough."

Rafe moved in and kicked out, catching the
man in the gut, then yanked his arm forward,
turning his bulk into an ally.

With momentum and his own size used against
him, the man was propelled forward and face-
planted onto the concrete parking lot. He didn't
stay down but jumped up, murder in his eyes.

Rafe followed through by driving the heel of
his hand under the bridge of the man's nose.

Blood spurted, fast and heavy. It wasn't life-
threatening, but it distracted the man long enough
to give Rafe another moment to check on Shannon and her foe. The man wasn't as large as
Rafe's, but his bulk paralleled that of a defen-
sive lineman's.

She had done her best to keep him away from

Rafe, but he knew she couldn't keep it up much longer. How was he going to take out a second enemy when he was struggling to deal with the first?

Then his resolve hardened. He figured he had something the men didn't. They had probably not served in Delta Force, fighting in a down-and-dirty war where every day was an act of survival. More importantly, he knew the Lord was on his side.

He bunched his fist and slammed it into the man's temple. A glassy look filled the man's eyes before he toppled over.

Rafe didn't spare a minute's sympathy for him since his intent had been to kill Shannon and himself.

"You took care of yours like a pro," he said, impressed with her moves.

Shannon bent over at the waist to brace her hands on her thighs. Took a deep breath. Another.

"You all right?" Rafe asked.

"Never better." It was a lie, and they both knew it.

She withdrew her cell phone from her pocket and called 911.

Rafe pulled a couple of plastic ties from a pocket of his cargos and secured the men's hands. He then gently poked her bicep. "You've got guns."

She grinned. "I do, don't I?"

"Remind me not to make you angry."

"I think you're safe enough."

Sirens blared and lights flashed as the cops showed up and arrested the two men. Rafe didn't hold out much hope that the men would roll over on those who had hired them, but at least he and Shannon had gotten them off the streets.

She touched the skin beneath her eye, drawing his attention to the swelling that was even now beginning to show.

"That's going to be a real shiner," Rafe said.

She pumped a fist in the air. "My first."

He grinned at her, but his thoughts were grim. They had survived yet another attack, but how long could they keep this up?

NINE

"How'd you learn to fight like that?" Rafe asked on their way to the police station after making a stop at the ER.

Fortunately, her ribs were just bruised and sore. Given that they'd tangled with two heavy hitters, she and Rafe hadn't fared too badly. After their cuts and abrasions were treated and she'd been checked for a concussion, which she'd been fortunate enough to escape, they were given instructions to take it easy and released.

She was no match for someone like Rafe, who had had special-ops training, but she'd managed to hold her own in the fight and didn't mind admitting she was feeling pretty good about it.

"My brother raised me and wanted to make certain I could take care of myself when I went away to college. His goal was United States Marine Corps Force Recon, so he took as many training courses as he could, including Krav Maga, before he enlisted and then taught me every move he knew. By the time he left, I wasn't too shabby."

"Krav Maga. I thought I recognized some of those moves."

She shook her head ruefully. "Too bad I didn't remember to use those moves when that jerk held a knife at my throat." It still irked her that she hadn't fought back that night. Instead, she'd folded like a weak-kneed wimp.

"You were taken by surprise and were then in shock. Nobody's going to fault you for that."

"Except me," she murmured.

"Your brother did a good job training you."

Her brisk nod belied the heaviness that still weighed in her heart so many years after his death. "Jeff was one of the best. Everything I am, I owe to him." She read the compassion in Rafe's eyes. "I miss him every day, but I turned out all right."

"I'd say you turned out just fine." There was a rough quality in his voice that gave weight to the words.

She refused to read in anything more to that than the words themselves, but it was tempting to believe that they meant more than their surface value. And if they did? What then? She and Rafe had nothing in common outside of his assignment to protect her.

No man had captured her interest since her

fiancé had dumped her. Why now? Why Rafe? Granted he was off-the-charts handsome, but she'd known other good-looking men. He was also intelligent and courageous, and exuded integrity, but there was something more, something that went beyond normal appeal and reached down to touch her heart.

Enough of that. Rafe Zuniga was her bodyguard and nothing more. If she had any sense, she'd keep it that way.

Still, she couldn't tear her gaze away from him and covertly took stock of her protector. His dark eyes and the hard angles of his face gave him a no-nonsense air that shouted, "Don't mess with me."

But there was more.

He wore honor like a suit of armor. She read it in the steadfastness of his gaze, in the firm, uncompromising line of his mouth, in the hands that gripped the steering wheel with casual strength. Rafe Zuniga would never shirk his duty.

"Thank you for keeping me safe. Again."

"No thanks needed."

The big man didn't need anything or anyone to validate who and what he was. That made her like him all the better.

The trip to the police station and another round of questioning capped off an already long day. She wanted nothing more than to go home, get out of her suit and curl up in sweats. Right now, she was weary enough to fall asleep as she and Rafe exited the precinct and walked to his car.

He slid an arm around her waist. "No going to sleep yet. We still need to get you home."

She leaned in to his arm more than she would have liked. She, who had always prided herself on being self-reliant, was coming close, dangerously close, to leaning on someone else. She hadn't done that since Jeff had left to go overseas.

She straightened and inhaled deeply. The Colorado night was chilly despite it being August. She was not a woman who needed a man to prop her up. She was strong and capable and…a yawn escaped quickly followed by another. She clamped a hand over her mouth but was unable to stifle yet another yawn.

In the car, seat belt strapped around her, she did her best to stay alert, but exhaustion dragged at her until she gave way to it and slid into sleep.

Rafe heard Shannon's breathing even out. He shifted his gaze and studied her profile. Stripped of the tough DDA image she normally projected, she looked young and defenseless. She was pale enough that he imagined he could pass his hand right through her. He tucked a stray strand of hair behind her ear.

She'd fought alongside him tonight with all the

courage of one of his Delta brothers. Though he'd ordered her to get out of there, she'd entered the brawl without hesitation.

He'd never forget the bravery with which she'd stood up to a man twice her size. She was the total package—courageous, intelligent and so beautiful that she took away his breath.

The direction of his thoughts pulled him up short. He had no business thinking of Shannon in these terms.

Keep your mind on the job. The self-directed order had little effect, though, when he heard her sigh and took in the softness of her face in repose. He'd have liked to stay the night and guard her himself, but he knew his body needed sleep, so he called a female operative.

He thought of what Shannon had shared of her family. Her voice shone with love when she talked about her brother.

At Shannon's house, a small Craftsman tucked in a cul-de-sac, he pulled into the driveway. She woke when he turned off the motor. "Rafe?" She looked about. "I'm sorry. Did I sleep all the way home?"

"And snored."

"You're making that up."

He smiled. "Maybe." He let himself out and rounded the car. When he opened the passenger-side door, he started to lift her out of the seat, but she stopped him.

"I can walk."

"Your choice." He would have liked to carry her, to hold her close in his arms, but he sensed she needed to show that she could make it on her own.

Inside, she disappeared into the kitchen and within a few minutes returned with two tall glasses of lemonade. "Coffee will keep us awake."

She sat and patted the seat beside her. "You know everything about me. Tell me something I don't know about you."

"Don't laugh."

"Why would I laugh?"

"In high school, I thought about becoming a musician. Turns out that I was pretty good on the violin. My music teacher suggested I pursue it." Why was he telling her this? He'd never shared it with anyone outside the family.

"Why didn't you?"

He laughed self-consciously. "Look at me. I'm way too big to be a musician."

"What does size have to do with it?"

"Musicians have a look to them. I didn't fit."

"That's dumb."

"Maybe. That's what my mother said. But at the time, I was sure I'd be laughed out of Juilliard." Just as his Delta teammates would have laughed their heads off at the idea of him playing the violin.

Shannon didn't laugh. Instead, she looked at him with quiet understanding. And that was why he'd told her. He'd known instinctively that she wouldn't laugh.

She whistled. "You were accepted into Juilliard?"

"I was close," he admitted. "At the last minute, I knew I couldn't go through with it. An army recruiter came to our school and asked us if we were brave enough to help win the war on terror." He shrugged. "That was it for me."

She nodded her understanding. "I get it. It wasn't that you were too big to be a musician. It was that you wanted to keep America safe. Being a soldier is what you were meant to do."

Embarrassed now, he ducked his head. "That's not how it was."

"You can't fool me, Rafe Zuniga. You were meant to be a hero. And you were." She paused. "In my eyes, you still are."

"You have it all wrong. I'm no hero." He shifted in the seat. "A hero is someone who does something that wasn't expected. I did what I had to. What any man in my unit would do."

"I say you're a hero. And I'm the client, so that makes what I say right."

He laughed. "I can't argue with that kind of

logic." His expression sobered as he thought of the real heroes in his unit, men who had never come home. Losing buddies in the war was not unusual, but that didn't diminish the grief he'd felt upon each death.

That grief was magnified a hundred-fold when he'd returned to the States. Once he'd completed rehab, he'd wanted to continue his service but wasn't able to be deployed again.

The army had assigned him to deliver the news to family members whose son or daughter, or husband or wife, wouldn't be returning. In vivid detail, he remembered his hand raised, ready to knock on the door and say the words that would forever change the lives of those inside.

He carried with him the faces of those who stared at him first in disbelief, then in a pain so profound that they were all but buried beneath the rubble of it. Their faces changed as their world collapsed. The people they'd been before his fateful arrival no longer existed. When a death occurred, more than one person died.

Her expression troubled, Shannon looked at him. "Rafe…what is it?"

He shared the recollections, watching as sorrow shadowed her eyes.

"You're the most courageous person I've ever known," she said softly.

That was the last thing he wanted. "I'm not even close to courageous. If anyone is, it's you."

"What makes you say that?"

"It's the way you see your work. You don't see it as a job. You see it as a mission. It's the same with Deltas. Delta Force operatives don't have jobs. They have missions. Like you."

"Thank you. That's the nicest thing anyone's ever said to me." Soft color flooded her cheeks. Silence stretched between them until she broke it. "I want to have another go at the other shop owners. Maybe if they know what happened to Mrs. Kimball, they'll be more likely to step up."

Rafe wondered about her ex-fiancé. Had he not said nice things to her? And if not, why? He wanted to ask that question when a knock sounded at the door. He drew his weapon, then opened the door.

A female operative stood there. "I'll take over," she told Rafe.

Both chagrined and relieved at the interruption, he nodded. "I'll pick you up at eight in the morning," he said to Shannon.

"I'll be ready."

He let himself out.

As he drove back to his place, he admitted what he couldn't deny any longer: he had feelings for Shannon. He also had issues with trust, and he guessed Shannon had her own. Neither one of them was ready to trust, which meant that neither was ready to love.

TEN

Shannon had rented a meeting hall the following night for an hour and had invited the shop owners to attend. She had to try once more to convince one or more to testify. So as not to attract attention by having the people leave their businesses during the day, she'd arranged the meeting for night. Dusk had already come and gone, leaving a few determined stars to compete with the city lights.

Rafe checked out the room, then motioned for her to come in. People straggled through the doorway in small clumps of twos and threes. Furtive looks were cast about as though those who were there didn't want to be noticed.

Shannon stood at the front of the room. "Thank you, everyone, for coming."

From the undercurrent in the room, the shop owners were scared and nervous and no more willing to talk with her than they had been weeks before. Still, they'd shown up, and she seized on that as a good sign.

She'd thought of approaching the people separately, but had decided instead to do it in a group, hoping that courage from just one individual would affect the rest. She'd seen it before—the contagious quality of valor, that someone would decide to not back down no matter what. Surely there was one such individual among the group.

"You've heard what happened to Mrs. Kimball," she said, raising her voice to be heard over the rising wave of voices. "More than ever, we need to stop the men doing this. To do that, I need your help."

"You want more of us to be beat up?" a woman challenged. "Charlotte Kimball almost died. What I hear is even if she lives, she'll never be the same."

"You're asking too much," a man said. "If they'd do that to Charlotte, they'd do it to any one of us. Or our wives or our children. We can't take that risk." He shook his head. "Some of us have heard about a highway being built and figure that someone's looking to make a killing on it. We can't fight it. Not when our families' lives are at stake."

"We're sorry," a fortyish woman said. "But we're afraid. As for myself, I'm selling the business. It's not worth it." Tears shone in her eyes.

"Five years ago, I took over the store from my parents. They started more than forty years ago. Some years were lean, but they didn't give up. Someone tried to burn them out once, but they rebuilt." She chuffed out a breath that was more sob than exhale. "But I can't fight this. Not any longer. I'll walk away with a little profit. I guess that's something."

From the tone of her voice, though, it wasn't enough to give up something her family had built and tended for more than four decades.

"Do all of you feel the same way?" Shannon asked.

Everyone present nodded.

Shannon had to try one more time. "I understand how you feel, but—"

"Do you?" one man challenged. "I hear that you're single, but pretend for a minute that you have a family. How would you feel if you got a picture of your little girl with a bull's-eye on her chest? That's what came in the mail yesterday." He held up the picture with the unspoken but chilling message.

"I'd be terrified," Shannon admitted.

There were grudging nods at her honesty, but it didn't stop people from filing out.

Shoulders drooping in defeat, she gave Rafe a tired smile as they put away the chairs she'd rented. The shop owners were adamant against helping her, even more so than the last time she'd talked with them.

"I don't know what I'm going to do. Mrs. Kimball isn't able to testify. The others are too scared. And I don't blame them," she said, her spirits sagging along with her shoulders. "How could I?"

"Neither do I. They aren't equipped to fight Newton and his men."

"What am I going to do?" It seemed natural to share her problems with Rafe. Over the last few days, he'd become far more than a bodyguard. He was a friend.

"The lady who spoke last mentioned she was selling her store. I'd be interested to see who the buyer is."

Shannon slapped her forehead. "I should have thought of that."

"You would have. You'd just been dealt a blow, but you're back. What say we do some digging and find out who's buying properties?"

A call to the lady in question netted the information that an LLC had made the offer on the store and that the deal would go forward at the end of the week. Shannon thanked the woman and started calling the other shop owners. They had also received offers and were going forward with the sales, albeit reluctantly.

She called the first woman back. "Hold off as long as you can and ask the others to do so, as well. We're not beaten yet," she said, then ended the call.

Shannon turned to Rafe. "We're on to something."

"You're amazing."

"You're the one who came up with the idea."

"Okay. We're both amazing."

Shannon and Rafe left and headed to his truck. On the windshield, a white envelope was tucked in a wiper. Rafe opened it and read it, then handed it to Shannon. From the tightening of his mouth, she knew she wasn't going to like what she saw.

Her lips tightened as she looked at the letter. "'You've been warned. Mind your own business or we'll mind it for you.'"

She wanted to tear the paper into shreds, but, instead, folded it and slipped it back inside the envelope.

"There probably aren't any fingerprints, besides ours, but I'll have it tested just to be sure."

Rafe's expression was grim. "Only cowards leave anonymous notes. It's not too late to back off, let someone else take over."

"We've been through this before. I'm not backing off. I'm not backing down."

"I know."

Not for the first time, she wondered what she'd

gotten herself into, but it was the first time that she feared she might never get herself out.

Rafe didn't bother making small talk on the way to Shannon's home. He understood she was processing. So was he. If the woman had any sense at all, she'd bow out of the case and let someone else from the DA's office take over.

"You know I have to do this," she said when he pulled into her driveway.

"I know. Doesn't mean I have to like it."

"No. If you want out, I understand. I know I'm not making things easy for you."

He gave his first smile of the evening. "Ain't that the truth? Like I said before, my grandpappy would say that you're stubborn as a Missouri mule."

"Why not a Colorado mule?"

"Colorado mules are far less stubborn."

"Really? You've made a study on that, have you?"

"Of course. Studying mules was part of Delta training." His eyes grew serious, the teasing gone. "You've stirred up a hornets' nest. It's not going to go away."

"I didn't stir up anything. But I plan to light a fire under those particular hornets. I'm not going to let them loose on innocent people. Not on my watch."

"You're pretty amazing."

The warmth of Rafe's gaze rested on her, yet she resisted the urge to squirm under it. "No. People like Mrs. Kimball are amazing. I'm just one more DDA trying to do their job."

"A DDA who risks her life seeing that justice is done." The words were warm, causing her heartbeat to quicken.

It was time to get back to work. She needed to go through her trial strategy. Again. And she couldn't do that with Rafe hovering over her. He was too distracting, too appealing, too everything.

Shannon knew herself well enough to understand that she was falling for the handsome body guard. That was a mistake. She had too many trust issues to fall for him, or any man for that matter. Look what had happened the last time she'd given her heart.

Rafe was everything a woman could ask for in a man. And too appealing by half.

When he looked at her with those darker than dark eyes that seemed to reflect everything in their fathomless depths, she forgot that he was her bodyguard and started thinking of him as something else.

"I'm staying the night," he said, interrupting her flow of thought.

She gave a smart salute. "Yes, sir."

"I'm sticking to you like glue on a fly strip."

"You do have a way with words. Maybe you should write greeting cards."

"Maybe I should."

At last his mouth tilted upward, and she wondered why she had been so eager to see him smile. He was too handsome, too everything for her peace of mind as it was. When he smiled, his appeal rate went off the charts. She had no business thinking about Rafe that way. She had no business thinking about him at all, except in his role as her bodyguard.

Yeah, right. Try telling that to her heart.

She shook her head as though the gesture alone would clear away the punch of attraction she experienced whenever she was in Rafe's presence. It didn't. She chewed on her bottom lip. When this was over, he'd exit her life as quickly as he'd entered it. Why was she so depressed at that?

He was her bodyguard. Nothing more. Nothing less.

Rafe had quickly discovered that the workday didn't end for Shannon once she was home. On the contrary, she continued working far into the night.

He watched as she read through a report, her tongue caught between her teeth. A tiny wrinkle worked its way between her eyebrows. He'd come to recognize the expression whenever she was deep into what she was reading.

She was so involved in her reading that she didn't even notice when he disappeared into the kitchen and rummaged through the cupboards and refrigerator. When he returned, it was with plates of grilled-cheese sandwiches and sliced tomatoes.

He set a plate on the coffee table. "Take five minutes and eat."

"You're always trying to feed me."

"And you're always forgetting to eat." Could she tell that something was weighing on him besides her poor eating habits?

Shannon lifted her head. "You're worrying how to tell me something."

"How'd you know?"

"Reports aren't the only thing I can read. Your face is an open book." She reached out to touch his hand. "You're a good man. You care about your clients. You care about people. But you don't have to worry about me."

"Whatever happens, I'll keep you safe." He prayed he could make good on his promise. He cared about her. There. He'd admitted it. But it went no further than that.

His track record in the romance department was dismal.

She pressed Rafe's arm. "I know you will. I'm

always safe when I'm with you. In the meantime, I have a job to do, more cases to work."

"What do the other attorneys do? Seems like you're doing everything."

She laughed. "Hardly. At any given time, we may have up to forty, even fifty, cases pending. We each do our share."

"I'd have thought that, given the Newton case, you'd be exempt from taking on others."

"I wish. And I wish the case wasn't as bad as others I've seen. But I can't let it go. The shop owners deserve better." Her sigh was part exhaustion, part disgust. "Right now, I'm prosecuting a man for robbing the home of a seventy-eight-year-old woman. But that wasn't enough for him. He also pistol-whipped her.

"If I get what I want, he'll go away for a long time. Right now, he's out on bail. But that won't last, once we go to trial and get a conviction."

"You're positive."

"I have to be. If I let the horrors I see every day get me down, I'm afraid I'll never get up again." She wet her lips, took a long breath. "I can't let that happen."

"What keeps you going?"

"Knowing that I can make a difference. If I can protect the next person from a man who beat a seventy-eight-year-old woman, I'll be satisfied."

He let his gaze take in the absolute conviction in her eyes.

"We're not so different," she said. "We each want to make the world better. One day at a time."

"You're pretty special, you know that?"

"I'm no more or less special than anyone else trying to do their job."

"What happens if someday there are no more bad guys for you to prosecute? What will you do then?" He didn't really believe that it was a possibility, but he'd wanted to make her smile, and to that end, he'd do or say anything.

"Then I'll know I did my job really well." She laughed. "I'm not going to worry about it. I don't see much danger in the world running out of bad guys." Her lips drooped for a second before lifting again. "In the meantime, I'll keep doing my job and you'll keep doing yours.

"As long as you're standing with me, I'm safe."

Her faith in him was touching. But what if he wasn't there when she needed him? What if he messed up? What if he...? Rafe shook his head, negating the scenarios.

As a friend in the SEALs had said on more than one occasion, *Failure is not an option.*

Rafe clenched his jaw. Newton would have to go through him to get to Shannon. And he wasn't budging.

ELEVEN

The old-time diner should have been comforting, with its original gray Formica and red vinyl stools and booths, but Shannon couldn't shake the depression that had been her constant companion ever since her trip to the hospital to see Mrs. Kimball.

Tucked in a picturesque canyon leading up to the mountains, the diner was located on an old road that led to popular ski resorts. A recently constructed highway bypassed the diner, leaving it largely empty.

She'd arranged to meet Harold Post, a shop owner, at the small diner outside the city. Like him, she wanted to make certain that they weren't seen together. It had taken all of her powers of persuasion to get him to agree to that much.

From everything she'd learned about him, he was a good man. He took care of his family, including elderly parents. He was active in his church and served at a community soup kitchen.

Rafe had taken a seat at the back of the diner, where he could keep an eye on everything and everyone.

"You saw what they did to Mrs. Kimball." Post clenched and unclenched his hands. "Next time they go after someone, they're likely to kill 'em. I've got a wife and three kids, plus parents who depend on me. I can't afford to take that risk." He dipped his head for a second before raising it to give her a shamefaced look. "I'm scared. I almost didn't come today, didn't want them following me to see that I was meeting with you. I don't like admitting that. It goes against everything that's in me, but it's the truth."

"If all of you stood up to Newton and his men—"

Post shook his head. "Just stop right there. We can't go up against them. They aren't afraid to break bones, or even kill. What are a bunch of shop owners going to do against men like that? Most of us have never even held a gun, much less fired one."

"There's strength in numbers. I could arrange police protection for you." The words sounded as weak as they felt.

"Didn't you do that for Mrs. Kimball? Lot of good it did her. 'Sides, the police aren't going to stick with us every minute of the day. No, ma'am. I can't do as you ask. I wish things were different, but they aren't. I have to think of my family. If that pack of hyenas got their hands on one of my kids or my wife or my mother..." He shook his head. "I can't risk it."

Shannon couldn't blame him or the others. Newton had done a good job of scaring everyone silent.

"Thank you for coming today, Mr. Post. I know it wasn't easy. If you change your mind—"

"I won't."

He slid out of the booth and walked away. When she'd first met him, he had carried himself with an air of pride and dignity. Now his jowls sagged, along with his shoulders.

Rafe joined her in the booth. "No go?"

She nodded glumly. "He's right. I can't ask him to stand up to Newton's crew, not after what they did to Mrs. Kimball. He has too much to lose."

Taking her elbow, Rafe walked her out of the diner, allowing her to talk through her feelings. "You've done everything you could to get someone to testify."

"It wasn't enough. And if you're going to try to convince me to drop the case, save your breath." She lifted her chin. "I don't run."

"There's no shame in running."

"Like you've ever run from anything in your life."

"I've run from plenty. Like a warlord in Afghanistan who wanted my head on a pike. I laid low for a while, until my team and I were in a position to capture him. He was taken to stand trial for war crimes."

"But you didn't really run. You just waited for when the time was right to get him. I can't run from this," she said. "I have to see it through. For Mrs. Kimball. For all the others." Her voice turned steely. "And for anyone who has been a victim of someone who thinks he's above the law."

They came to a stop at his truck, where a white envelope was anchored beneath a windshield wiper. Rafe pulled a pair of plastic gloves from his pocket and slipped them on before pulling the paper free. He undid the envelope, looked at the note and scowled.

Shannon leaned in and saw what had caused his frown:

Come to the Point if you want to get the goods on Newton.

The Point was a tourist attraction, a formation of rocks shaped like an arrow point located twenty miles outside of town.

"A setup," Rafe said flatly. "No way are you going."

"I have to."

"If it's legitimate, whoever sent this would have delivered the message in person."

"I have to go," she repeated. "With you or without you."

He didn't say anything more, only helped her inside the truck, then climbed inside himself and headed west of town. The drive, through a narrow two-lane highway, took almost forty-five minutes.

They didn't talk, for which she was grateful. She knew Rafe was angry with her, but it couldn't be helped. She only hoped that she'd made the right decision.

When they reached the landmark, Rafe pulled the truck into a small parking lot marked Visitors and turned to her. Whatever he'd been about to say was lost in a popping noise, which resulted in a neat little hole in the windshield.

Automatically, he pushed Shannon down. They'd been set up. He didn't bother berating himself for walking into a trap. He had to get Shannon out of here.

He flung open the truck door and threw himself outside, then crab-walked around to the passenger side and opened the door. Motioning for Shannon to stay down, they half crept, half crawled to a stand of trees.

Shots were being fired all over the place. Either the shooter was an extremely poor marksman, or he wasn't trying to hit them. It didn't matter: a stray shot could kill just as easily as a deliberate one.

He listened as one shot after another pinged, trying to decide where the shooter was. Finally, he got a bead on the location.

"Stay put," he said.

For once, she nodded without asking a lot of questions. Only one came forth. "What are you going to do?"

"I'm going to get behind the shooter."

"You can't just go out there with no cover."

"No choice. As we are, we're pinned down, and we've got no way to get out of here." He handed his clutch piece to her. "Do you know how to use this?"

She accepted it, reluctance heavy in the gesture. "Yes."

"Good. Don't shoot unless you have to. But don't be afraid to use it. Your life may depend on it."

He noticed that those last words had her squeezing the weapon more tightly. "Let me come with you. I can help."

"Not this time. Stay low and stay alive."

Shannon crouched lower to the ground.

He inched backward, keeping flush to the ground. When he judged it safe, he got to his knees, listened again, then stood and, giving a wide berth to where he thought the shooter was positioned, circled around behind.

There. In the brush and crouched behind a boulder. A figure dressed in camouflage. He looked and then looked again. His heart rate dropped as he stared in disbelief.

Daniel Kimball held a shotgun to his shoulder, his hands placed too far apart for control of such a powerful weapon.

More disgusted than angry, Rafe walked up behind him. "Put down your weapon and stand up slowly."

Rafe wasn't surprised when Daniel did as he was instructed. The young man was unaccustomed to holding a weapon, much less using it.

"Turn around."

Once again, he followed orders.

Rafe picked up Daniel's weapon in his left hand. "What do you think you're doing?"

Daniel spat. "Getting justice for my mother."

"And shooting Ms. DeFord is your way to do that?"

"I *have* to do something. My mother is still in a coma. The doctors don't know if she'll ever recover."

Rafe patted the man down, looking for any other weapons. "And you blame Ms. DeFord for that?"

"Yes."

"What about the men who beat up your mother? Don't they deserve at least part of the blame?"

Daniel looked down, shuffled his feet. "I don't know how to get to them. And that attorney convinced my mother to testify. If she'd left things alone, everything would have been all right."

"Do you really believe that?" Rafe challenged.

"Why shouldn't I? My mother's a good woman. She's worked hard all her life. She didn't deserve what happened to her."

"For once, I agree with you. But taking it out on another innocent woman, one who hasn't done anything to you, isn't the way." Rafe ran his gaze over the man with undisguised contempt. "You're a coward. Almost as much of a coward as the men who put your mother in the hospital."

Daniel raised his head, puffed out a narrow chest. "I'm no coward."

"No? What do you call shooting at an unarmed woman?"

Daniel stood as tall as his slight stature allowed. "I call it justice."

"You're a coward," Rafe said again. "And foolish along with it."

Shannon joined them. The shock in her eyes was quickly replaced with sorrow.

"What do you want to do with him?" Rafe knew what he'd like to do with Daniel. His sympathy was all with Mrs. Kimball, not her wea-selly son.

"Hold him while I call nine-one-one."

"You'd do that to me, knowing what you did to my mother?"

"I don't have a choice," she said, her words heavy with sorrow. "You could have killed some-one by shooting at me here."

Rafe heard the regret in her voice, but Daniel didn't. He shot her a look of pure dislike.

"Your mother is a good woman, and I don't want to see her hurt unnecessarily, but this can't go unpunished. I'm sorry. For her sake. She has enough to deal with without finding out that her only son is a fool."

She and Rafe waited for a black-and-white unit to pick up Daniel. "You did the right thing," Rafe said when the officers had cuffed him and driven away.

"He was reckless, and he broke the law, but I feel sorry for him."

"You're not like any prosecutor I've ever met," Rafe said with a shake of his head.

"Mrs. Kimball has suffered enough. And her son is right—I am to blame. If I hadn't pressed her—"

Rafe sliced a hand through the air. "You're too smart to fall for that."

"Maybe. But right now, I can't help feeling responsible."

He took her by the shoulders. "You were doing your job. Nothing more. So stop blaming yourself."

"You're right." She shook away his hands. "But I owe Mrs. Kimball, so I'll keep doing my job and stop Newton and whoever's behind him."

Shannon couldn't help feeling sorry for Daniel, even though he'd chosen a foolish path. His mother was in the hospital, perhaps never to walk or talk or even breathe on her own again. She started to say something, then bit it back.

"Go ahead," Rafe said. "Say what you want to say."

"Thank you."

He looked surprised. "For what?"

"For keeping me safe. For being here."

"Why are you so determined to prove yourself at this job? Why is nailing Newton and his men so important?"

"Because it's the right thing to do." There. That should satisfy him.

"Because it's what your father failed to do. And you won't let yourself be like him. No matter what the cost."

She jutted out her chin. "And if that's true? What of it?"

"You need to decide what's right for Shannon DeFord. Right now. Not fifteen years ago."

She gathered all the disdain she could muster. "You don't know what you're talking about."

"If I don't, then you don't have to worry about it." He gave her a moment, then added, "The past won't leave you alone until you decide to leave it alone."

What kind of gibberish was that? "I don't know what you're talking about."

"Oh, I think you do. I think you're so enmeshed in what your father did—in how he abandoned his principles and then you—that you can't think of anything else."

"That's ridiculous."

But it wasn't.

She hadn't dealt fully with the pain of her past. Until she did, she couldn't move on. Did moving on include Rafe? Or was he only a passing phase?

That's when it hit her, that everything she'd done since her father had run from the job and then accepted bribes had been to prove that she wasn't like him, that she could and would stand and fight. The past would continue to haunt her as long as she allowed it to.

Rafe had been right all along. She'd been too blind, too stubborn, to see it. "You're right—I haven't fully faced the past. But first, I have to deal with the present. And that means stopping Newton."

Could she do that? At one time, she was certain she could and would face any challenge. Now she wasn't sure. At all.

TWELVE

Shannon had a lot to think about as Rafe drove her back to the office. Not the least of which were her feelings for her handsome bodyguard.

Mere physical appeal, she could have ignored, but Rafe offered so much more. He'd stuck by her with each new danger they faced. Duty and honor defined him in every word and every action. It wasn't just that he'd been in Delta Force that made him who he was. It was something intrinsic to the man himself.

She had no business thinking of him in anything but a professional manner, but it was impossible to ignore the effect he had on her. *Focus on the case.* That was where her energies needed to lie. And hadn't she already given this lecture to herself? Little good it had done.

She feared she was irreparably damaged, starting from the time she was a child and her parents abandoned her, leaving behind a kind of void that had followed her all of her life, despite everything Jeff had done, all the way up to her fiancé choosing a fancy lifestyle over her.

She had only three years under her belt at the DA's office. She wanted to move forward, not for the sake of power but for the city and its people. She loved Shadow Point, but the city wasn't without its faults. Many of those faults had to do with corruption within the system. She wanted to weed out dirty cops, kickbacks and fraud, and make the city shine as it was meant to.

Shadow Point was her home. For Shannon, that said it all. A distant memory intruded on her mind. She and Jeff had just moved into a new apartment. He was working full-time, and she was still in school. The first thing her brother had done was carve a plaque that read Home is Where They Love You No Matter What and then he'd hung it over the front door. Neither had had that with their parents; both had been determined to make it so with a fresh start.

She snuck a glance at Rafe, saw the grim set of his mouth and guessed he was thinking of Daniel. At that moment, a muscular-looking pickup truck T-boned Rafe's vehicle.

Their truck went spinning, doing a full 360 in the middle of the highway. When it stopped, Shannon heaved out a huff of relief that she and Rafe appeared to be in one piece.

That relief was short-lived when a barrage

of bullets cut through the air. Rafe grabbed her hand, and together, they scrambled out the passenger-side door.

"Stay low," Rafe shouted.

The continuous spitting of bullets sounded like they were coming from a dozen MP5s, but Rafe detected only one metallic crack of a slide blowing back and slamming forward. That was the good news; the bad was that the man firing at them seemed to have an unlimited number of bullets and could keep them pinned down indefinitely.

Rafe blocked out the fear and focused on what needed to be done—namely, getting behind the man and getting the drop on him. To do that, he needed to stash Shannon somewhere safe. He scanned the area behind them and found a rock cropping that offered a fair amount of concealment.

"There," he shouted.

He half pushed, half dragged Shannon behind the rocks. "You'll be all right if you stay here."

"Where are you going?" The words were almost lost in the constant blasting of bullets.

"To nab us a bad guy."

Scrabbling through the rough vegetation and rocks, he circled widely behind the man shooting at them. The erratic shots indicated the shooter wasn't trained with such a weapon and was only firing countless rounds in the hope that one would find its mark. And one would, given enough time.

Rafe didn't intend on giving the man any more time. So intent was the shooter on his task that he failed to detect Rafe belly-crawling toward him. Rafe grabbed the man's ankle then pulled him down. His weapon fell from his hands.

The two men wrestled on the ground until the goon pulled a knife from an ankle holster. Rafe could have pulled his weapon at that time and shot him, but he wanted the man alive.

On top of Rafe, the man had the knife poised at Rafe's chest. At the last second, Rafe rolled, and the deadly blade caught his arm.

The sound of ripping cloth told its own story. Then came the pain, dark and treacherous, as it ripped into him, much as the knife had shredded the sleeve of his shirt and torn into his flesh.

Despite the throbbing in his arm, Rafe grabbed a hold of his foe's wrist and bend it backward. His assailant let out a scream and released the knife.

Rafe got to his feet, pulling the man up with him. He tightened his hold on his opponent's wrist, stopping short of breaking it, then he eased up. "Who sent you?"

A shake of the head was his only answer.

Rafe started up the pressure again until the man cried out, "Enough."

By this time, Shannon had joined them. She tore a sleeve from her own shirt and wrapped it around Rafe's arm, despite his shooing motion to her. He didn't have time for that.

"I'm fine," he said between clenched teeth.

"If you're fine, you won't mind my tightening this a bit." She gave a tug on the torn sleeve.

His grimace negated his words. "Let me see to this creep, then you can doctor me all you want." He pulled flex-cuffs from his pocket and secured the man's arms behind his back. "Let's try this again. Who sent you?"

"I don't know."

"Not a good answer. Try again."

Another shake of the head. "Honest. I don't know. There's a contract posted on the lady on the dark web. A hundred K for the person who offs her. I figured, why not me?"

For a moment, Rafe wanted to rail at the unfairness of it. The enemy seemed to have infinite resources, leaving him and Shannon at a distinct disadvantage.

He leaned forward, letting his size intimidate the shooter. "The dark web?"

Shannon's revulsion at the words traveled down Rafe's spine to become his own. The dark web wasn't easy to navigate, and once you went down it, you came away feeling like you need to take a month's worth of showers.

The man gave a jerky nod. "Yeah."

"How do we find the post?"

"How should I know? I ain't no computer genius or nothin'."

"You had to know something to get to the contract," Shannon pointed out, receiving only a glare in answer.

Rafe groaned. His arm ached, but the pain was bearable. Right now, it was more important that they get any information they could from the man.

"Why? I told you what I know. Can't you just let me go?"

Rafe and Shannon exchanged can-you-believe-this? looks. "Believe it or not, attempted murder is against the law. You're going to jail. You're going to tell your story to the police and you're going to sit in a cell until arraignment. And if I have my way," he said, voice hardening, "you'll be sitting in a cell for a good long time after that."

"No harm, no foul."

"You were going to murder the lady and me. Seems only fair we return at least part of the favor."

The man spat. "No wonder you two is on someone's bad side. You got no sense of fair play."

"You call coming after us with a gun and a knife fair?"

"It weren't personal." He said the words as though they excused what he'd tried to do. "It was just business."

"That makes it all right, then." Sarcasm hung heavily in Rafe's response.

"Really? You're gonna let me go after all?"

"No." Rafe speared the man with a look of disgust. "We're not going to let you go. You're going directly to jail. You will not pass go. You will not collect two hundred dollars. Got it?"

When the man only glared at Rafe, Rafe punched him in the arm. "I repeat—got it?"

"Got it." Resentment oozed from him. "You ain't gonna be so high and mighty when those who want you dead get a hold of you and the lady. They play for keeps."

"And how would you know that? I thought you didn't know who hired you."

Flummoxed, the man gulped, then stared down at his feet. "You're trying to trick me."

"No. I'm just pointing out that you're a bad liar. Normally, I'd count that as a good thing, but in your case, I think it's just because you're not smart."

"I'll show you smart."

"Oh? And how're you going to do that?"

The man puffed out a puny chest. "Maybe I

know stuff that you'd like to know. But I ain't talking."

"Funny. Seems like you've been doing plenty of that."

Shannon gave the man a dismissive look. "You're right, Rafe. He's not smart enough to know anything useful. Nobody would trust him with any real information."

The man smirked at Rafe and Shannon, probably as close to a smile as he was capable of giving. It didn't soften his features. If anything, it emphasized the darkness in his expression as the smirk grew into an ugly sneer.

Rafe needed to get his arm looked at, but first he had to see to this fool. "We're going to see that you spend some quality time behind bars."

"You got nothin' on me."

"How about attempted murder? Two counts. I'm sure we can think of some other things while we're at it." Rafe turned to Shannon. "What do you think?"

"Oh, I think we can come up with something. Like threatening the life of a deputy district attorney for one and trying to kill both of us for another."

Rafe tapped in 911 on his phone and gave the location. "Your ride will be here in a few minutes," he told the man.

When two black-and-white units showed up, Rafe gave a brief explanation.

They drove to the ER, where he had his arm seen to. Outside the hospital, Rafe and Shannon sat in their vehicle. They needed time to regroup.

"You sure know how to show a girl a good time," she said. "What's next?"

Though he appreciated her attempt to lighten things up, he knew she had to be scared out of her mind. Having a contract put out on her for any lowlife to try to cash in on was a terrifying proposition. He reached for her hand and squeezed it. She sent him a grateful smile in return.

His arm began aching, but he was loathe to use the painkillers the ER doctor had prescribed. From previous experience, he knew they made him groggy and could slow his reaction time. He couldn't afford either.

She rested her head against his shoulder. "I've tried to keep up a good front, but I'm scared." She lifted her head, gazed at him straight on. "There. I said it."

"Didn't come easy, did it?"

"No."

"Being scared is nothing to be ashamed of. Some of the bravest soldiers I served with were upfront about being afraid of going into battle. It was those who said they weren't scared that I worried about. Either they were lying or they weren't smart enough to know what could happen, and that meant I couldn't trust them or their reactions."

"Try being the DDA whom everybody's avoiding like the plague. I'm beginning to feel like Typhoid Mary. They know that it could be any one of them who could have been tagged for the case and become a target."

"Plague and typhoid? You're mixing your diseases," he said, trying to get a smile from her.

"You're right." But the smile he'd hoped to coax out didn't materialize. "When I took this job, I promised myself that I wouldn't back down. No matter what. Now I'm wondering if I can keep that promise."

He had some idea of what it cost her to say the words. "It'll be okay."

"Will it?"

He took her hand and gently squeezed it. "Nothing's going to happen to you. Not as long as I'm here. It's gonna be okay."

"Promise?"

"Promise. You're an amazing woman. But you already know that."

"Thank you for not saying 'I told you so.'"

"Why would I do that?"

"You told me that things would get worse before they got better. You were right."

The quaver in her voice homed in Rafe's attention to her face. Exhaustion dragged at her. He saw it in the tiny lines fanning the corners of her eyes, in the drop of her shoulders. He wanted to tell her to take a few days, to leave the job to someone else, but he knew he couldn't.

"I know what you're thinking. You're trying to find a way to get me to back off. Again."

"Guilty."

"Thanks for not saying it. You're the one who should back off. You've been shot at, nearly blown up by a bomb, run off the road and stabbed with a knife, but you've never complained."

He tipped an imaginary hat. "All in a day's work."

"Seriously, Rafe, you didn't sign on for this."

"I signed on to do the job. The job means keeping you safe."

She clapped a hand over her mouth to stifle a yawn. "I can never repay you for what you're doing."

"You can repay me by staying alive." His voice had roughened. When he saw the hurt in her eyes, he regretted it.

"If you want out—"

"Do. Not. Go. There."

"Guess we're stuck with each other then."

"Guess so." He slung an arm around her shoulders, careful to keep the hug friendly.

"I promised to keep you safe, and I'll do my

best to keep it." Rafe added a silent prayer that he could make good on his promise.

Shannon felt as though she was breaking apart in a million pieces, far too many to put back together. Would she ever be whole again? At this moment, she doubted it. She doubted she'd ever be able to find the pieces of herself, much less find where they belonged and fit them into the proper places.

Maybe she didn't want to. Maybe she should look for a new order, a new kind of wholeness.

Right now, she didn't feel strong enough to even lift her head from Rafe's shoulder. Nor did she want to. She wanted to stay where she was, safe in his arms, head nestled against his shoulder as she absorbed his strength.

Reason returned, and with it, a measure of pride. Slowly, reluctantly, she pulled back. "Thank you."

When her cell buzzed, she looked at it, saw the detective's name.

"Ms. DeFord? Detective Lannigan here." About to tell him that they were just on their way to see him, she halted at his next words. "I wanted you to hear it from me before you got wind of it some other way. Newton's been murdered."

Not certain she'd heard correctly, she asked him to repeat what he'd just told her.

"Shot twice in the head," he said, finishing up. "A couple of hunters found him." He gave the location and told her he'd be in touch.

Shaken by the news, Shannon put down the phone.

Rafe looked at her in concern. "What is it?"

"Newton's been murdered. Some hunters stumbled across the body."

"How?"

"Shot." She exhaled a long breath. "It's not like anyone is going to miss him."

"Someone was afraid you were getting too close."

She nodded. "That's what I thought. Taking out Newton ended that trail. I wanted to take him to trial, to have him face what he's done."

"What's our next move?"

She liked that he had automatically ranged himself with her. "Thanks."

"For what?"

"For being on my side."

"Always." His smile came quickly, then disappeared just the same. "Newton's death doesn't mean you aren't still a target. Whoever killed him is getting desperate."

She'd already thought of that.

"If I had my way, I'd take you out of state,

stash you somewhere safe where nobody knows you and wait this out. But I know that's not going to happen."

"I have to see this through." They'd had this discussion before, and, she admitted, she was tempted to do just as Rafe said. She didn't fool herself into believing she was indispensable. Another DDA could take over the job. It would take a while to get him or her up to speed, but it could be done.

It wasn't pride that kept her from running; it was fear. She needed to be able to trust herself. If not, there was no way she could keep doing her job or anything else.

"I know." He shook his head ruefully. "I had to try."

"Thank you."

"For trying to get you to leave the job to somebody else?"

"No. For caring enough to try."

The look that passed between them was one of mutual respect and something more. It was that *more* that had her worrying her bottom lip with her teeth. With more effort than it should have taken, she reminded herself that she had good reasons for not wanting to take the relationship any further beyond that of bodyguard and client.

Then why was she daydreaming about something more between them?

Admitting that she was scared—terrified, even—had been one of the hardest things Shannon had ever done, but there was relief in the words. She didn't have to keep up the brave act. It was growing thin, and she was having a harder and harder time convincing herself that she wasn't afraid.

Not for the first time, she wondered what she'd gotten herself into, but it was the first time that she feared she might not get herself out. "I want to go to the murder scene."

THIRTEEN

"You what?" Certain he had heard incorrectly, Rafe stared at Shannon.

"I want to go to where they found Newton. I need to see the scene for myself. Maybe we'll see something the police missed."

"They aren't likely to miss anything. Anyway, it's going to be a zoo there once the press gets hold of it."

"I've been to crime scenes before."

"This is different."

But Shannon wasn't going to be dissuaded. With a couple of calls, she arranged for Rafe to accompany her to the crime scene, and they made the winding trip up a narrow canyon to the foothills north of Denver, where Newton's body had been found. If not for some hunters, Rafe doubted the body would have been discovered so quickly.

Unexpected patches of color, brought on by cooler temperatures in the higher altitude, en-

hanced the otherwise gray-and-green landscape.
A gray sky cupped the jagged edge of the mountains.

When they reached the site, Rafe parked on
the side of the road, only getting that far because
Shannon had shown her credentials to the officers who were turning away any vehicles going
beyond a certain point. After rounding the truck
and opening her door, Rafe took her elbow and
helped her across the boulder-studded ground.

The mountain setting made it more difficult to
breathe. Though he had been born and raised in
Colorado, even he was not immune to the higher
altitude.

A cheerless rain added to the atmosphere of
gloom, shrouding the already morbid scene in
a misty gray. Thick branches of towering pines
provided minimal protection from the rain that
could easily turn into snow. Birds called from the
tree line. A cold wind stirred the damp air and
brought with it the scent of pine, but beneath it
was the smell of death. Raw and recent, it clung
to the air, a smear that wouldn't vanish.

Someone had had the foresight to bring a couple of heavy-duty flashlights, which cast eerie
halos around people's heads, adding to the macabre nature of the proceedings.

"You're sure you want to do this?" Rafe asked,
hoping she'd changed her mind.

"No. But I'm sure I have to." Her voice was as resolute as her squared shoulders.

Police and crime techs from the ME's office went about their jobs in a choreographed series of movements that said that each had performed the dance many times before. Once again, Shannon was required to show her credentials before she and Rafe were allowed on the scene.

With latex gloves on his hands and cheeks reddened by the wind, Detective Lannigan greeted them. "I thought you might come, Ms. DeFord."

"I appreciate you letting me know about it." She made introductions. "Detective, Rafe Zuniga, my bodyguard. Rafe, Detective Lannigan."

The men acknowledged each other with a nod.

"It's a nasty day for viewing death," the detective said and swiped at the continuous stream of rain that dripped down his forehead.

She held his gaze. "Any day we're looking at murder is nasty."

Rafe noted that Shannon's face had paled, but she wasn't turning back. Not that he'd thought she would.

"There is that." Lannigan gave another swipe of his hand. "Can't say that I'm sorry about Newton's death. He was scum. Still, I didn't want to see him taken out this way."

"Neither did I."

Rafe studied Shannon while she studied the scene. She'd refused an umbrella and rivulets of raindrops made their way down her face. She appeared not to notice, intent only on learning what she could. Despite the gruesome circumstances, she was holding up.

He'd expected no less.

"Ballistics will do their thing," Lannigan said, "but I don't expect we'll get a match. Whoever did this is too smart to have used a weapon with a history."

"Does the ME have a guess as to the time of death?" Rafe asked.

"She says around three to five this morning. She'll have a better idea when she gets him on the table."

Rafe had met the ME during another case. Though she was at least twenty years his senior, they had clicked and had become fast friends.

Doris Dunnaway was a single mother and didn't put up with any nonsense, from police veterans to her seventeen-year-old son, Jonah. When Jonah had been picked up for joyriding in a stolen car, she'd called Rafe and asked for help. After learning that he had gone along for the ride, not knowing that the car was stolen, Rafe had been able to talk the owner out of pressing charges. He'd then given the boy a frank talk about where he was headed if he kept on that same path.

He moved a few feet away to where the ME was hunkered over the body. "Doris," he said.

She looked up and gave a wide smile, her face wreathed in the spotlight of the bright lights. "Zuniga, what brings you here?"

He jerked his thumb at the body. "He did."

"What's your interest in him?"

"He's part of a case I'm working on."

"From what I hear, he was a real jerk, but he'll get my best."

Rafe didn't doubt it. Doris didn't care what her "patients," as she called them, had done in life; she cared only what they told her in death. Finding the truth drove her.

A muted pain spread from his upper arm all the way to his fingers. He made a fist, trying to control the soreness.

Doris must have noticed his grimace and the way he held his arm close to his chest. "What's going on with your arm?"

"Took a knife to my upper arm. Barely more than a sting." The ache in his arm said differently, but he ignored it and focused on learning whatever he could.

"Knowing you, you're probably not taking anything for the pain, are you?"

"Don't need it."

Doris gave him a who're-you-trying-to-fool? look but didn't say anything more. "Whoever did this was cold. I'll be able to tell you more after I get him on the table. For now, you get what everyone else gets." She looked up briefly. "You probably already guessed. He wasn't killed here. This was only the dump site."

"Thanks."

She shifted her gaze to where Shannon stood talking with the detective. "Is she the case you were referring to?"

"Yes. Do you know her?"

"Shannon DeFord. I've met her a couple of times. Dedicated and too good for the likes of Hamilton Brooks. He'll work her until she drops and then claim credit for anything she accomplishes."

It was a strange comment, as Doris wasn't one to gossip about people in the law-enforcement community, but Rafe didn't get to follow up on it, because Shannon and Lannigan were approaching.

"Thanks, Doris," he said as Shannon and the detective joined them.

Rafe angled his body to shield Shannon from the worst of the wind.

"Your boy was killed execution-style," the ME said, directing her remarks to Lannigan. "Looks like a nine mil."

"Someone was sending a message."

Rafe nodded. Newton hadn't been a choirboy by any means, but he hadn't deserved being killed in such a manner.

Shannon kneeled beside the body,

Rafe heard the little gasp she gave. "What is it?"

"He has the same tattoo on his arm as the man who attacked me in the courthouse."

Rafe leaned in closer. "The serpents. Looks like a prison tat."

"You're right," the detective agreed. "Makes sense that he and one of his boys would have the same one."

"You hadn't mentioned that until now," Rafe said to Shannon.

"I'd forgotten. Or maybe I'd blocked it out of my mind. But I remember it now." She shivered. "I remember it very well."

"Just because Newton's dead doesn't mean you're out of danger," Lannigan told Shannon. His voice was hard, but his eyes held a trace of sympathy. "Whoever wants you dead likely still does. Getting rid of Newton was step one in cleaning house."

"Newton was only the hired help," Rafe said.

The detective's terse nod confirmed that. "That'd be my guess. None of his crew would be willing to take him out, so that leaves someone else calling the shots."

Would Shannon be willing to step aside now,

after she'd seen the violence those behind Newton visited upon anyone who stood in their way? Rafe was mulling over suggesting once more that she let someone else take over the case when she aimed an I-dare-you look his way.

Wisely, he kept his thoughts to himself.

The danger to Shannon had risen exponentially. Whoever was behind this was cleaning house. Getting rid of Newton had been the first step.

With him dead, the case would go back to the cops so they could find his killer and determine if it was attached to something bigger. For Rafe, it had become more important than ever to discover the assailant and the person behind everything if he wanted to keep Shannon alive.

Newton as a threat had been identifiable. Now the threat didn't have a face or a name.

Protecting her had just become a whole lot harder.

Shannon knew Rafe was worried. She was sorry for it, but it couldn't be helped.

The trip back down the mountain occurred in near silence. Her ears popped the farther they descended, and she shook her head to rid herself of the sensation.

Though she'd spent all of her life in Colorado, she still suffered from the occasional bout of altitude sickness if she ventured too high. There'd been no skiing trips for her, though Jeff had offered more than once.

As it always did when she thought of her brother, her heart hiccupped a little bit of pain. At the same time, a headache formed at the base of her neck, and she massaged gently, hoping not to attract Rafe's attention.

At last they reached Shadow Point. Without asking, Rafe swung by a drive-through place and picked up sandwiches. "Eat something. It'll help with the headache."

She hadn't mentioned it, but he'd picked up on it nonetheless. He was extraordinarily sensitive, which unnerved and warmed her at the same time.

She gave him a grateful smile. "Thanks."

When they reached her office, she didn't object to his precautions in checking it out before he let her inside.

She spent the next hour revising the case she'd present in court.

Just as he stepped out of the office to go to the restroom, the phone rang.

She answered with a distracted "Yes?"

"If you care about your bodyguard's life, you'll stop your investigation." The call was disconnected after the last word.

She stared at the phone as though it could alone

provide answers. She immediately contacted Detective Lannigan, who was quickly able to tell her from the number that it had been made from a burner and that tracing it would take time and resources. When he asked what it was about, she gave a noncommittal answer, thanked him and hung up.

She couldn't put Rafe at risk. It was one thing to risk her own life, another thing to put Rafe in danger. Granted, he'd been in danger while protecting her, but this was a direct threat against him. Grateful that he was out of the office for a few minutes, she struggled to come up with a way to convince him to drop the case.

He'd made it clear that he was in it for the long haul. Maybe if she told him that she believed she was out of danger, despite the detective's words, he would take the hint and move on.

Over the last few years, her career had exposed her to some grisly scenes, but she'd gotten through them, believing she had her fair share of courage. Now, she accepted that she was as vulnerable as the next person when it came to knowing someone she cared for was at risk, especially since it was because of her.

When Rafe returned from the restroom, he gave her a frowning look and folded his arms across his chest. "What's wrong?"

"Nothing. I've just been thinking that I'm

wasting your time here. Lannigan's warning not-withstanding, I think I'm out of danger. I can't afford to keep you on the clock for any longer."

"I thought we'd already settled that. S&J is picking up the tab."

"I pay my own way."

"Shannon." He rounded the desk and put his hands on her shoulders, urging her to stand. "What's really going on?"

"Nothing," she repeated.

"You're a poor liar. Now tell me the truth."

She averted her gaze. "I have. It's not polite to accuse a client of lying."

"No, it's not. That's why you're going to tell me what has you running scared."

She should have known she couldn't fool him. "There was a call and…"

"Now we're getting somewhere. Did the caller threaten you?"

"Not me," she said carefully.

"Then who…" He stopped. "I get it. He threatened me. Right?"

Miserably, she nodded. "I can't risk you. I won't."

He closed the space between them. "You're not risking me."

"I didn't know what to do," she murmured. "I've put you in danger."

"Hey, that's my job, remember?" He put a

small distance between them, just far enough that they could look at each other in the eye. "I can take care of myself. Or haven't you noticed?"

Of course, she had. "But you're a target now, same as me. If something happened to you…" She couldn't continue. The images in her mind were too horrible to contemplate.

"Nothing's going to happen to me. If you think about it, I've been a target all along because whoever is after you has to go through me. Nothing's changed. Don't you see? This is a ploy to make you easier to get to. Without me, you're vulnerable."

"I don't care. Not if it costs your life."

"You aren't thinking straight. Whoever called you was counting on that. They want to frighten you so that you'll make a careless mistake, like getting rid of me. When you get over being scared, you'll see that and realize that nothing has changed. I'm here, and I'm not going anywhere."

She wanted to cry. Not out of fear, but out of gratitude. Still, she couldn't make Rafe a target. "You're a good man, but I won't sacrifice you. Not for this."

"You're not sacrificing me." He cupped her shoulders. "Look at me. You're a brave woman who has been through more than anyone should have to endure. You'll keep doing your job, and I'll keep doing mine. It's as simple as that."

"Promise me you won't take any unnecessary risks."

He fit a finger beneath her chin and raised it. "That's what I'm supposed to say to you."

She pushed away from him. A woman could only take so much, and despite every effort to keep them at bay, tears rose in her eyes. She wished with everything in her that it was too dark for Rafe to see them.

"It's going to be okay," he said. "You're worn out." He held out his arms. "Come here." He folded her into his arms and held her as carefully as though she was made of fine porcelain.

It had been a long time since someone had offered her genuine comfort. Not since Jeff, had anyone cared enough to hold her, to wipe away her tears.

How did she explain that the act of wiping away her tears had touched her in inexplicable ways? She could have handled it if he'd told her to buck up, to quit acting like a spineless wimp, but she was defenseless against simple kindness.

And, for the first time in too many years, she let go. She let go of the rigid control with which she'd held herself together and let loose the pressure that had been building within her.

Tears fell in droplets, then in a torrent, accompanied by hiccupping sobs. These were not the pretty, glistening tears as seen on celebrities who occasionally indulged in a delicately staged cry. These were messy tears along with noisy gulps of breaths that she would surely regret a short time later.

She cried for her brother. For her parents. For her ex-fiancé, rat though he was. Mostly she cried for herself and the shambles that had become her life. She let Rafe hold her and felt the reassuring beat of his heart as he cradled her head against his chest. All the while, she listened to the quiet cadence of his voice as he promised her that everything would be all right. Somehow she believed it, believed him.

"Go on. Get it all out. You'll feel better for it. You've held it in for too long."

His urging just made her cry harder, causing a tremor to rattle through her.

When she was certain she couldn't shed another tear, she gave a watery laugh. "You asked for it."

"You needed to get it out. Anybody would."

"I can't see a big strong Delta like you breaking down and crying all over someone."

"Don't be so sure. I cried plenty when I was deployed. I cried at what I'd seen, images I'll never be able to rid myself of."

She looked at him with new understanding for

him and shame for herself. How had she dismissed what he'd been through as though it was nothing?

She pulled away far enough to take in his soaked shirt, now streaked with her tears. "I've ruined your shirt."

"My shirt's seen a lot worse than a few tears." He didn't seem at all upset about it.

"Has it?"

"It has." He withdrew a perfectly pressed handkerchief from his pocket and handed it to her.

She used it to wipe away her tears, then refolded the square of linen. What did she do with the used handkerchief? She couldn't just give it back to him. Vainly, she looked for a pocket in her skirt and realized she didn't have one.

"Don't worry about it," Rafe said, then took it from her and stuffed it in his pocket. The casual way he handled it eased much of her mortification, and, for that alone, she was grateful.

Why did men's clothes always have pockets and women's have none? She'd think about it later.

"Thank you," she murmured. "Letting a client cry all over you wasn't in the job description."

"I signed up to take care of you. This is just part of the job."

The job. How could she have forgotten? "Of

course." She pulled away from him. She didn't need Rafe or any other man to prop her up.

"Speaking of jobs," she said, "it's time I got back to mine."

"You will. In a minute. First, you need to take a deep breath and remember that you're not alone. I'm in this with you, and I'm not going anywhere." He paused. "The Lord is on your side, too."

She might be just a job to him, but she was still glad he was on her side. The reminder was a steadying one. As for the Lord being on her side, it was something to think about. She didn't trust herself to speak and only nodded.

"You're stronger than you know," Rafe said.

Was she? Right now, she felt piteously weak. "Where were we before my little meltdown?"

"I was promising you that I'd keep you safe and that I'd do the same for myself."

"Maybe we should promise to take care of each other."

"I like the sound of that," he said, his voice a caress. "I like it a lot."

So did she.

Look how he'd cared for her when she had fallen apart after the phone threat. He'd held her as he would a child, let her soak his shirt with her tears and, later, had dried those same tears.

Never once had he berated her for what she saw as weakness. Instead, he'd praised her strength.

That kind of compassion was rare.

She couldn't tell him that. He would deny it and say it was all part of the job. He would have to come to it in his own time, on his own terms. In the meantime, they still had bad guys to take down.

She braced her spine along with her determination. *Do your worst*, she silently vowed to those trying to keep her from doing her job. *You won't stop me.*

FOURTEEN

"Sorry about earlier," Shannon said. "I don't usually break down like that."

Rafe shook his head. "You're entitled to a few tears after all you've been through."

"Thanks. But that's not who I am. It's not who I want to be."

"Don't apologize for being human."

Her vulnerability hadn't lasted. He could almost feel her defenses shift back into place. He didn't blame her for it. As they said, been there, done that. He had his own shields so firmly erected that nobody got through.

Why, then, did he feel the shield slipping a bit? Was it because of Shannon? He'd served as bodyguard to other beautiful women and had never been drawn to them as he was to her.

So what was different this time? Was it that Shannon had gotten to him in a way no other woman, including his ex-fiancée, had? Despite his best efforts to convince himself that they couldn't have a relationship for professional reasons, he knew it was more than that. Much more. He couldn't be with any woman until he learned to trust again.

Rafe had to put this case to rest, and he had to do it fast before he lost whatever sense he possessed.

When Doris released her findings on the shooting, he read through the autopsy report on Newton. It wasn't complicated. Two shots from a 9 mil to the forehead. Death was instantaneous.

A gangland execution.

Despite the tat on his arm, Newton's record didn't show traditional gang affiliations. He was the head of the crew that had terrorized shop owners, but he didn't belong to any of the established gangs that were proliferating at an alarming rate in the Rocky Mountain west.

So why the gang-style execution?

Was it to throw off law enforcement from the real cause of his death? That was Rafe's take on it.

There were no ballistic matches to the gun used to kill the man. That could mean anything, including that the killer was savvy enough to use a gun that had never been put in the system.

Rafe knew they were getting closer. He felt it. Call it intuition or a gut feeling, but he knew they were closing in on the head of the operation. They just needed a few more pieces of information to make everything fit into place.

Sometimes finding the truth wasn't so much finding the right piece of the puzzle, but eliminating all the wrong ones.

"The key to this whole business is following the money," he said.

"I thought we'd already figured that out. The money goes to whoever buys the land." Shannon let out a long sigh that spoke of exhaustion and frustration.

"That's small change. The big money goes somewhere else. Or, I should say, someone else. Who stands to benefit the most if the highway goes through that area?"

"Whoever owns the land."

"Wrong. They'll benefit, sure, but it's chump change compared to the contracts handed out for construction of the freeway. Materials. Labor. We're talking serious money here."

"How much is serious?"

"We're talking in the tens of millions. Maybe hundreds."

Shannon's eyes widened. "You have to be joking."

"No joke. Highway construction is big business, big enough to attract organized crime. Think about it. Material costs alone are huge, and then there're the labor costs. That means labor unions. Unions can mean the mob."

Though most labor unions were honest and operated for the good of the workers, some had been infiltrated by organized crime.

"We need to go to the hall of records," she said.

Shannon and Rafe spent the next hours going through every document related to the issuing of construction contracts they could find. Dozens of contracts made out to various companies showed up. When they dug further, they found many of the companies were shells.

"I think I've got something." Excitement crackled in Shannon's voice. "Here." She pointed to a number. "This number turns up in every contract. Sometimes it's a phone number. Sometimes it's a shipping number. Sometimes it's something else. But it's there. Every time."

They studied the string of numbers, trying to make sense of them, but none could be linked to a social security number, a phone number, passport number or any other common number.

On her tablet, Shannon used an app to assign letters to the numbers. Now they had a string of letters that still made no sense. "Maybe it's an anagram." She moved the letters around, did it again. On the sixth or seventh time, she said, "Look."

She and Rafe stared at the name, then at each other. Albert Calhoun.

"Would he be so egotistical to use the letters of his own name?" she asked.

Rafe rubbed his chin. "In my experience, men who've gotten to where Calhoun has aren't lacking in ego."

"We need to pay him a visit." She laid a hand on Rafe's arm. "We've got to be careful. If we're right about him…"

"After all that's happened, careful's all I'm going to be." Rafe tried to find a reason to keep Shannon from going but nothing came up. He exhaled loudly. "Why do we say we want to see him when we get there?"

"Albert Calhoun owns the biggest construction company in the state," Shannon said thoughtfully. "Given his friendship with my boss, I think he'd be willing to give us some insights on the industry."

"Let's do it."

They made the trip to downtown offices of Calhoun Construction and, after giving their names to the front desk, were shown into the big man's office.

The office was opulent in the extreme. Everything from the desk—a slab of live-edge walnut polished to a high sheen—to the paneled walls shouted money. Lots and lots of money.

Rafe supposed that in an industry where contracts ran in the hundreds of millions, image mattered. Like the killer view of the Rockies from the window. Though Shadow Point didn't boast a dominant skyline, the profile of mountains jutting into the sky like jagged teeth made for an impressive backdrop. And though he was hardly an expert on art, he recognized the oils that graced the walls. No prints allowed here.

A framed quote snared his interest. *Citius venit malum quam revertitur.* Four years of Latin in prep school enabled him to translate it. *Evil arrives faster than it departs.* Interesting choice, especially among the fine artwork.

"Ms. DeFord." Calhoun then turned to Rafe, who offered his hand. "Zuniga, isn't it?" Calhoun reached out to take it, steely fingers biting in a little too deeply, revealing information that his mouth had not.

Interesting.

Calhoun gestured to a couple of chairs.

Shannon and Rafe took seats designed to be uncomfortable, a common practice among busy people who discouraged lengthy visits.

"That's right," Rafe said easily, his gaze caught by the ring on the man's pinky. Two serpents intertwined on the large gold center. A glance at

Shannon told him that she'd noticed the same thing and that the significance hadn't been lost on her. "You have a good memory."

"What can I do for you folks?" Calhoun asked.

"Mr. Calhoun, thank you for seeing us. We need some insights into the construction industry for a case I'm working on," Shannon said, "and hoped you could help us."

Calhoun sat back in his chair and folded his arms across a bulldog chest. His manner was expansive. "You came to the right place."

"What can you tell us about how contracts are awarded?" Rafe asked.

Calhoun went into a long spiel about the process of awarding of construction contracts. Nothing he said was something they couldn't have learned with a Google search. After spending a half hour pontificating, Calhoun leaned forward and propped his elbows on his desk. "I hope that helps."

"Very much so," Shannon said and stood. "Thank you for sharing your expertise with us and for your time."

"You have any more questions, you just shoot them over to me," he said and pressed a button.

A receptionist appeared and saw Rafe and Shannon out.

They talked of inconsequential things as they

took the elevator down to the lobby level and walked outside.

"You saw the ring," Rafe said.

"I noticed it when we met at the fundraiser, but I didn't get enough of a look at it then to see the serpents."

"I'd say that was more than a coincidence," he said. The sun shone brightly, and he blinked. With his hand shading his eyes, he almost missed movement in a nearby doorway, where a man trained a gun on them. He pushed Shannon to the ground and drew his weapon at the same time.

A bullet hissed by him, followed by the thud of running feet.

He helped Shannon stand. "Are you okay?"

"As okay as I can be after being shot at. What about you?"

"Same." He gave her a long look. "You know what this means?"

"Calhoun signaled someone when we were leaving." Twin lines bracketed her mouth.

"Let's get you out of here."

They hustled to the truck. After checking it out for explosives and anything else—he wasn't taking any risks—he opened the passenger door.

Most of the trip back to her office was spent in silence. He figured they were both processing what they'd learned. After wrestling with his conscience about what was the right thing to do, he said, "Calhoun being in on this puts a new spin on it. A man like that has unlimited resources. If one of his hired guns is taken out, he can hire fifty more."

Rafe focused on getting her to listen. "I promised I'd keep you safe. The best way to do that is for you to step away. I'm doing my best to see you don't get hurt, but I'm afraid my best isn't good enough."

That apparently got through to her. "Why would you think that?" she asked more softly now. "You've put yourself in the line of fire over and over in protecting me."

"And almost gotten you killed in the process. Some bodyguard I am."

"You're up against people who will stop at nothing. There's nobody I'd rather have at my side. So why—?"

"Why do I keep reminding you that there are others who can do the job of going after Calhoun and his henchmen? That you aren't indispensable?"

"Yeah."

"Because you care so much about the case that you put yourself in danger every day. Others wouldn't care so much, wouldn't make themselves a target."

"I can't be anything except what I am," she said quietly.

"I know." And, truthfully, he wouldn't want her to be.

"You sound like that's a bad thing."

"No. Just the opposite."

"Can't you see, Rafe? I need you on my side, fully committed. I have to do this. For Mrs. Kimball. For the other shop owners. If you're not with me, then I'll go at it alone. But I won't stop."

"I know. But I won't let you put yourself in danger. If I say no to something, you accept it."

Keeping Shannon alive meant he had to keep every fiber within him focused on that goal. He couldn't afford to let down his guard. Not for a moment.

They had good news and bad news. The good news was that they now had a name for the person behind the attacks. The bad news was that they had not a shred of real proof against him.

FIFTEEN

Back in her office, Shannon paced the length of the room, more disturbed by the discovery about Calhoun than she wanted to admit. She knew he was involved. She felt it in her gut. If only they had more proof to back it up.

If she and Rafe were right about Calhoun, it explained a lot of things, like the number of trucks the enemy had had at his disposal. It made sense that a construction company would have multiple pickups, not to mention burly men to send after them. And, lastly, how an assassin would know that she and Rafe would be coming out of Calhoun's office at just that time.

In her mind, she replayed the conversation she and Rafe had had with Calhoun. She let out a long, frustrated sigh. "We have to take him down. There's no telling what other pies he has his fingers in. He could be running groups like Newton's all over the state. The whole West."

"I'm sure he is," Rafe agreed. "The kind of organization and planning something like this takes wouldn't be used only once. There's a sly kind of meanness to it, preying on the most vulnerable of business owners. Newton and his organization wouldn't go after a big business. They'd strike at those who can't fight back, who'd eventually give up because they didn't have the resources to keep up the fight."

"You sound sure about this."

"I am. I saw the same kind of thing in Afghanistan, when the warlords would go after a small village, one without enough men to resist. After a short while, the villagers would give in because they'd lost too many people. Others heard what was going on and gave in before the fighting ever started."

Shannon shivered. "What makes some people so vile that they'd use their power that way?"

"Ego. Greed. A need for more and more power, no matter the cost, no matter who gets hurt. The businesses in Shadow Point are only the tip of this. When we dig deeper, we'll find more small businesses being forced out, whether by violence or some other means."

"We have to stop it," Shannon said. "This can't go on."

"He's not going to be easy to take down," Rafe responded. "He has friends in the state capital. And beyond."

She had to tell her boss. Brooks needed to know that Calhoun was tangled up in the case. She expected he'd reject the idea at first, but he'd eventually come around. Brooks put the job first. Always.

It was early evening, but she knew he would still be in his office. Like her, he kept long hours.

"I need to tell my boss," she said to Rafe. "He needs to know what we suspect."

He frowned. "Maybe I should go with you."

"I'll be in the DA's office. What can happen to me there?"

Brooks's secretary saw her into the office.

He disconnected a call and put down his cell phone, impatience in his eyes. "Yes, DeFord, what is it?" His wired state set her own nerves on edge.

She'd planned on easing in to it, but realized that wouldn't soften the blow of learning that his friend and biggest financial supporter was part of a conspiracy of murder, greed and corruption. "I think Calhoun is part of what's been going on," she said without preamble.

"What are you talking about?"

Step by step, she went through what had brought her and Rafe to that conclusion.

"That's it?" The boredom in her boss's voice bordered on contempt.

That set her hackles rising. "Isn't that enough?"

"All you've got is some suppositions and not much else."

"I've seen you go after a case with less," she pointed out.

"Albert Calhoun is *somebody*," he said. "You don't go accusing the richest man in the city, probably the whole state, of corruption without real proof."

"We'll get it. I just wanted to give you a heads-up."

Brooks stood, placed his hands on his desk and leaned over it. He aimed a hard look her way, causing her to take a step back. "You're way off base," he said in a low, intimidating voice.

"I know Calhoun's a friend, but—"

"But nothing. Direct your investigation else-where. That's an order. Now, if there's nothing else…" He turned his back to her, a clear dismissal.

She started to leave. That's when she saw it. The intertwining serpents that bordered the quote that had snared her interest on her last visit to the office, though she hadn't paid attention to the snakes at that time. The same serpents tattooed on the knife-wielding assailant's and Newton's arms. The same serpents engraved on the gold center of Calhoun's ring.

A fizzy feeling of awareness prickled the hair at the nape of her neck. It was nothing but a coincidence. Serpents were a common enough symbol. No big deal. A coincidence, she told herself once more.

But hadn't she and Rafe used the serpents to connect Calhoun and Newton and his pal? They hadn't dismissed that as a coincidence.

She stared at the plaque a moment longer, cleared her throat and said, "I, uh... I'd better get back to work." A shudder of fear caused a quiver in her belly, and her uneasiness ramped up another notch. She stole another look at the quote, and the truth slapped her in the face.

The pieces clicked into place, the niggling feeling she'd had when she'd been in Brooks's office several days earlier.

Why hadn't she put it together before now? The serpent tattoo on the arm of the man who'd attacked her in the courthouse, the same tattoo on Newton's arm, the serpents bordering the words on Brooks's plaque and on Calhoun's ring. Maybe if she hadn't been scared for her life, she'd have made the final connection.

She had to get out of here before Brooks saw what she knew must be reflected in her eyes. She dug her nails in her palms in an attempt to even out her breathing.

Why hadn't she listened to Rafe? He hadn't liked the idea of letting her give Brooks the news about Calhoun on her own, but, as she'd pointed out, what could happen to her in the DA's office?

"Is something wrong?" he asked.

"No."

She started to leave, but he grabbed her arm and spun her around. "You saw something. What was it?"

"N-nothing."

"You're a bad liar, Shannon. Tell me what it was you saw." When she remained silent, he twisted her arm behind her back until she cried out as pain screeched from her shoulder to her fingers.

"The serpents bordering the plaque on your wall. Calhoun has the same ones on his pinky ring. That's all."

"Oh. I thought it might be something important. Like you put two and two together and came up with five."

"Nothing like that." She tried for a smile but winced at what she knew was a poor effort. "I have to get back to work if I'm going to find the answers I'm looking for."

He shook his head. "It's always the little things, isn't it, that trip you up? You just couldn't quit. You'd been given plenty of warning." He pulled a nine millimeter from his desk and pointed it at her chest. It was the same kind of weapon that had put a hole in Newton's forehead. "Wondering where I got that?"

Throat dry and hands clammy, she nodded.

"I have a guy at the security station who owes me. He smuggled it in for me." He stroked the nine mil lovingly.

"You killed Newton, didn't you?"

"He was a fool. Worse, he refused to follow orders and lie low until this all blew over. Finally, I'd had enough. Taking him out was ridiculously easy."

He spoke of murder the same way he might talk about improving his golf game, but that wasn't what was bothering her. Why was he confessing now, especially when she had so little to go on? He had no reason to tell her all of this, unless... Unless something had changed.

She had nothing to lose but to ask him straight out. "Why are you telling me all of this?"

"Because it doesn't make a difference anymore."

Confused, she could only stare at him.

"I did my best to keep you from digging your own grave, but you wouldn't let it go. I argued with Calhoun, telling him that you'd eventually come around. But you didn't." He pointed to his phone. "That was him on the phone. Seems that your little visit rattled him. He's tired of playing around and said to get it done."

"*It* being taking me out?"

"What do you think? You've got no one to blame but yourself. If you'd dropped the case, we wouldn't be where we're at right now."

"So it's my fault you're going to kill me?" she asked with heavy sarcasm.

"Why do you think I hired you? I wanted someone weak. Someone who would either give up or could be bought off. You refused to do either. You could have gone places if you'd been willing to cooperate."

She was still trying to wrap her mind around the knowledge that her boss, a man she'd admired, was part of the whole ugly business. How had she not seen or felt it before now? Things started to make sense, including his hints in the last week that she let someone else take over the case.

"Why else? I was grooming you to take over for me. With you in my pocket and Calhoun to finance things, I'd have everything I needed to run this burg. And from there, who knows how far I'll go?"

She kept her chin up when what she really wanted to do was to bawl like a baby.

"I figured you were holding out for the big one. This was a test, Shannon, and you failed. You failed miserably. Why do you think I assigned you the Newton case? You were supposed to botch it, and Newton would go back to what he was doing. At the very least you were supposed to drop the case. I thought you got that. I made it plain enough."

"What made you think I'd deliberately botch a case?"

"It was obvious. You left your big-shot job at that fancy law firm to come here. Why would you do that unless you saw the opportunity to make real money?"

"And you thought this because?"

"Because of your old man, of course. Why else?" He sent her a how-clueless-can-you-be? look. "We gave you every opportunity to drop the case, but you refused to see what was right in front of you. When it became obvious that you weren't going to cooperate, we tried to scare you off so we could replace you with someone who knew the score. But you wouldn't be scared.

"We even took out your witness, but you just kept going. Why couldn't you have been like your old man?"

"Sorry to disappoint." How long would her father's legacy hang over her? She thought she'd put it behind her.

"Not yet, but you will be."

"You must see that you won't get away with this."

"No? I've been getting away with a lot worse

for years. You think this is the first time I crossed the line?" He laughed, a cackling sound, and pushed his free hand through his hair.

"I had such high hopes for you. All you had to do was play it smart. Why couldn't you have dropped it?"

He shook his finger at her, looking for all the world like a bad-tempered child, red-faced and obstinate, with his hair standing on end. He was unwilling to listen to anyone who tried to reason with him. "Maybe because I have integrity." Angering him wasn't smart, but she couldn't help herself.

"You're a fast talker, DeFord. Too bad you're not smart along with it. I should have left you in that fancy law firm and hired someone who was more intelligent. Do yourself a favor, and play it smart now. Don't give me any trouble if you want to live a little longer."

She nodded, hoping that placating him would buy her time. Time to think of a way out of this. Time to stay alive.

It was the last thought she fixed upon. As long as she was alive, there was hope.

She put her hands at her sides, kept them loose, though she wanted to clench them into fists and knock him on his butt. The violent notion startled her. Before this case, she'd never wanted to physically hurt someone. First, the men who had attacked her and Rafe, and now Brooks. What was happening to her?

"You won't have any problem with me." That was the truth. The last thing she wanted was for someone to get hurt if Brooks started waving that weapon around.

"Okay. Let's go."

She refused to show that she was terrified. This was a man she didn't know, didn't recognize. She'd known he was ambitious, but she'd never suspected that he was dirty. How could she have been so blind? "What are you going to do with me?"

"You and I are going to take a little ride. One you won't be coming back from." He chuckled thickly.

He nudged her forward a few more feet before stopping, then removed a book from the bookcase and pressed something in the wall. The door opened. "This has come in handy more than once over the years. I could leave without being seen and my, uh, associates could visit the same way."

She pretended to stumble and flung herself backward, ramming the back of her head into his face. Pain sizzled through her at impact. In the confusion, she managed to rip off her necklace and let it fall by the door, hoping Rafe would see it and know that she was in trouble.

Brooks grabbed her and spun her around. "Think you're cute, don't you?"

She wouldn't cower from him and angled her chin. "Not really."

"Maybe this will wipe some of that misplaced courage from you." He backhanded her, sending her to her knees.

"You're a real gentleman, boss." She wiped the blood from her mouth and got to her feet. "You won't get away with this."

"So you said. Don't you have anything more original? As for getting away with it, I'll be just fine. You're not going to be around to testify. And I've got just the place for you."

With the gun at her back, she went down the stairs. At the bottom, he reached around her to open a door leading to the outside. He gestured to his car, pushed a button on his key fob and said, "Get in."

She did as ordered. "People know I came to see you. There'll be questions."

"And I'll say that we had a nice visit and that you left."

"You don't think anyone will notice that I never returned to my office?"

"I think people see what they're told. Who's going to suspect me of taking you? I'm the one who brought you into the office. I'm the one who championed you when others said you didn't belong. I'll be as distraught as anyone when it turns out that you're missing."

"Rafe will find me," she said.

"That so-called bodyguard." He punctuated each word with a sneer. "What do you expect him to do? He'll make some noises about finding you, but he'll be as baffled as everyone else. Because you're going to disappear."

"Disappear?"

"Yeah." He gave a nasty snicker. "You could say that you're going to go underground."

Then she got it. Calhoun owned construction sites all over the city. Brooks planned to kill her, then dump her body in one of the sites and cover it with dirt or cement. No one would be the wiser.

Or maybe he wouldn't kill her first. That was even worse. The idea of being buried under thousands of pounds of dirt terrified her. She bit back the scream that threatened to spew from her throat.

He gave her an approving nod. "I see you've connected the dots."

She didn't give him the satisfaction of begging, only stared straight ahead. She wasn't beaten. Not yet.

She knew Rafe would come for her. In the meantime, she would do whatever it took to stay alive. Her courage took a nosedive when Brooks pulled plastic ties from his pocket.

"Never know when these will come in handy," he said and yanked her forward by her arm. "Got them from a police buddy." He bound her wrists, taking savage pleasure in pulling the ties as tightly as possible.

"You made your choice. Now you have to live with it." He laughed. "Or, maybe I should say, you have to *not* live with it."

Rafe sensed that he and Shannon were close to fitting all the pieces of the puzzle together, but they weren't quite there yet. It felt like they were missing a key piece.

He put in a call to Tamra, the IT specialist at Colorado's S&J location, asking for anything that would link Calhoun and Newton.

Ten minutes later, his phone beeped. He snatched it up eagerly. "Did you find anything?"

"Five years ago, Newton worked on one of Calhoun's projects as a building foreman. He didn't last long. He was fired for stealing materials and falsifying billing labels. He was bound over for trial, but the charges were dropped."

Rafe waited. He knew from her voice that there was something more, but held his questions, knowing Tamra liked to tell things in her own time. "Something else. Hamilton Brooks, a DDA at the time, was slated to prosecute the case."

That was news to Rafe. Did Shannon know? Probably. She wouldn't have thought it a big deal, since many felons are repeat offenders.

"One more thing," Tamra added. "Calhoun's company is on the verge of bankruptcy. He lost money on the last three bids. Calhoun Construction plays in the big leagues, so you get the idea."

Rafe understood that the construction business was a high-stakes game, especially at the level where Calhoun played with make-it-or-break-it kind of risks.

After thanking her, Rafe hung up and pondered what he'd learned. So there was a connection between Calhoun and Brooks and Newton, *and* Calhoun's company was close to bankruptcy. His thoughts kicked into overdrive.

Anxious to share what he'd learned with Shannon, he grew impatient waiting for her to come out of Brooks's office. It was only supposed to have been a brief meeting, but it had lasted almost fifteen minutes. He should have insisted upon accompanying her to see Brooks.

He gave a perfunctory knock at Brooks's secretary's door. When he received a "come in," he opened the door and walked straight to the door leading to the DA's office and pushed it open.

"Wait! You can't go in there."

"Watch me." It took less than five seconds to

determine that neither Brooks nor Shannon was there.

How had they slipped past him?

Tension prickled the back of his neck, warning him that something was wrong. He'd learned not to ignore those feelings. They'd saved his life on more than one occasion.

The muscles of his belly tightened, just as they always had before he led a mission into enemy territory. He gave the office a more thorough study and noticed the plaque on the wall with the same quote as the one in Calhoun's office. The same serpents on Calhoun's ring bordered the quote.

Another coincidence? That was two coincidences too many.

Brooks was in on it. Brooks and Calhoun were in on it together.

Shannon had trusted Brooks, had gone to him with what they had. She'd had no reason to believe her boss was part of the conspiracy.

Rafe only prayed it hadn't cost her life. He had to find her before it was too late. He returned to the secretary's office. "Shannon said she was going to meet with your boss. She never came back."

The fiftyish secretary gave a startled yelp as Rafe slammed his hands on her desk and leaned over it, getting in her face. "I don't know, Mr.

Zuniga. Truly, I don't know. I saw Ms. DeFord go in, but I didn't see her come out. I figured she must have left when I was in the restroom."

The lady shrank in her chair, pushing it back toward the wall as far back as possible. "I don't know," she repeated, the last word ending on a wail.

"Okay. I apologize if I scared you." He searched Brooks's office again, more slowly this time. No sign that Shannon had been there. *Wait*. There was something gold on the floor near the back wall.

His long strides ate up the short distance. He stooped to find Shannon's necklace—the one she never took off—on the floor. A careful inspection showed that the wall wasn't really a wall at all, but a door. It fit so seamlessly into the wall that he would have missed it altogether if not for finding the necklace.

How did he access the door?

He pressed along the bookshelves, looking for some kind of button. Not finding any, he started pulling out books. When he came to *War and Peace*, he found a cleverly concealed button behind it. He pressed it, and the door opened.

He followed a short corridor until he came to a set of steps. It led to the bottom floor, where he found a steel door. One push and he was outside.

He retraced his steps, raced up the stairs.

"Brooks is gone," Rafe stated baldly to the man's secretary. He started to turn away, then thought of something. "What kind of car does your boss drive?"

"A Mercedes, I believe. Current year."

Impatience dug its claws into him. If Brooks was involved in Calhoun's dirty doings, it meant that Shannon was in the worst possible danger.

The secretary started to gather up her things. "I'm sure Ms. DeFord is all right."

But Rafe wasn't listening. Thoughts of what Brooks might even now be doing to Shannon wormed through his brain. He shut them down the best he could. Such images wouldn't help him find her and bring her back safely.

I trust you to keep me safe. Her words echoed in his mind.

He took a deep breath and forced himself to be calm, remembering what was at stake.

Shannon's life.

SIXTEEN

Bearing down on unspeakable fear, Rafe pulled his cell from his pocket and entered Lannigan's number.

"C'mon," he muttered as he waited for the detective to pick up.

When Lannigan finally got on the line, he barked, "What is it, Zuniga?"

"Brooks has Shannon. I know he's involved." Lannigan started to speak, but Rafe cut him off. He knew what the man would say: take it slowly. Be prudent. Tread carefully.

But Rafe was in no mood to take it slowly or to be prudent or to tread carefully. On the contrary, he wanted to act fast and act decisively. With as much patience as he could rally, he filled in the detective on what he and Shannon had learned, including the connection between Calhoun and Brooks and Newton, the serpents and how they'd been attacked when they left Calhoun's office.

"Do you know who you're talking about?"

Lannigan sputtered. "Calhoun's one of the most respected men in the state, the whole West. I can't arrest him for no reason."

"I'm talking about a man who orders murders like you'd order a cup of coffee."

"You know I can't do anything without more to go on," the detective said.

The lengthy pause told Rafe that Lannigan was taking a giant step backward. "As far as Brooks goes, you're talking about the district attorney of Denver. He's one of the most powerful men in the city."

"I know exactly who I'm talking about. Shannon's been missing for more than thirty minutes."

"Thirty minutes? That's nothing." In a more conciliatory tone, Lannigan asked, "What proof do you have?"

Once more, Rafe rattled off what he and Shannon had been able to accumulate. Even he had to admit it wasn't much, but it didn't take into account his gut, honed by years as a member of Delta Force, where his life and those of his men depended upon his instincts as much as intel fed to them by headquarters.

"I know he's involved. The longer you wait to act, the more likely that Shannon will end up like Newton."

"When you have something more than what your gut's telling you, get back to me. Until then,

I'm afraid I can't help you." The clipped response was followed by the sound of the call disconnecting.

Rafe called S&J and filled in Gideon, who had returned from special assignment, on Shannon's disappearance, including Brooks's connection with both Calhoun and Newton. "I don't know where to start looking for her." The second the words were out, an idea came to him. "Maybe I do. I'll keep you updated." He hung up before his boss could respond.

What was the first thing Brooks would do? Get rid of Shannon. What better way to do that than take her to one of Calhoun's construction sites? It would have to be an active construction site, yet one far enough out that they wouldn't be seen.

Fear rolled slick in his gut. He shook it off the best he could and marshalled his thoughts. Then he did what he should have done upon first learning that Shannon was missing.

He prayed.

"Lord, I let down Shannon, but I know You won't."

Shannon sat so rigidly in the front seat of Brooks's Mercedes that she felt she might shatter with every bump.

Too soon, Brooks stopped the car. He came around to the passenger side and hauled her out.

"You've been a real disappointment to me, De-Ford."

As he dragged her from the car, Shannon did her best to fight, but, with her hands bound, her efforts were futile. When she'd exhausted everything else, she raised her knee and kicked him in the gut with every bit of strength she could muster.

He didn't go down, but she'd hit him hard enough that he bent over and chuffed out a hard breath. "I could kill you for that, but I'll wait." He sent her a baleful glare. "Walk," he barked out and pointed straight ahead.

"Why don't you give up? You won't get away with this. Rafe will be looking for me, along with the police."

"No one's going to suspect the district attorney." He puffed out his chest. "It's too bad," he said with mock regret. "Together, we could have run this town."

"Once Rafe knows I'm missing and that you were the last person to see me, he'll figure it out."

"You put too much stock in that bodyguard of yours. How smart can he be if he turned down the opportunity to head up Allcott Mining?"

Surprised, she stared at him. "You know who his father was?"

"I know everything about the players in our fair city."

"Rafe doesn't care about money."

"Then he doesn't have the brains of a gnat."

"You wouldn't understand someone who isn't motivated by greed." The contempt she felt for him must have come through in her voice for he looked angry enough to spit nails.

"Shut up. You had your opportunity to be reasonable. You lost it. You have no one to blame but yourself for what's going to happen."

She saw from his eyes that he really believed that. Could she use his anger against him? Did she dare? He could retaliate in unspeakable ways. "Have you always been corrupt or is this a recent trait?"

"I've been using my office to pad my bottom line for years," he said without a trace of shame. "Why wouldn't I? My wife wears fur coats and designer clothes. My children attend the best schools. I buy a new car every year. Nobody gets hurt, and I'm living the life I deserve."

Was he serious when he said nobody got hurt? She thought of Mrs. Kimball, who was still struggling to breathe through a respirator, and the store owners who had been terrorized.

"You don't deserve to wear the title of district attorney. You betrayed the city and its people. You even betrayed yourself. You must have believed in what you stood for at one time."

A nonplussed expression appeared in his eyes,

and, for a fraction of an instant only, she saw regret in them. Was he remembering what it felt like to stand on the side of right?

Then he threw back his head and brayed in laughter.

"You're right. I didn't start off that way," he said in a self-righteous tone. "For the first few years, I watched embezzlers and crime bosses rake in the kind of money I'd never see as a public servant." He uttered the last two words with sneering contempt. "I decided to get some of that for myself. Once I learned how to grease the ropes, it didn't take much. A word here and a word there connected me with the right people.

"Did you really think you could sway me to give up everything I have?"

"And what would that be?" she asked, anxious to keep him talking.

"Money. Even more important, power. If things go my way, I'll be governor in a few months. A smart man can ride that all the way to Washington." Clearly, he considered himself plenty smart.

Until now, she'd held out hope that he might understand what he was doing by betraying his job and his principles. That hope died, with terror taking its place. Her mouth turned so dry that she could scarcely swallow. Finally, she worked up enough spit to ask one more question. "Are the money and power worth it?"

"Of course they are. You think I want to spend the rest of my life living on a civil servant's salary with nothing more to show for it than a pat on the back?"

"A lot of people do," she said.

"A lot of people are fools. Like you."

He was right. She had been a fool, but not for the reason he thought. She'd been a fool to think she could get through to him. "Why? Because I wouldn't roll over when you wanted me to?" She looked around and saw that they were at a construction site, as she'd guessed. Any attempt to run would end in failure—there were too many obstacles, including tools and holes to trip her up.

He pushed her along the rough ground to where foundation footings had been dug.

He shook his head at her. "You'd have been richer than you ever dreamed. It would have made what you earned at that fancy law firm look like peanuts."

"I didn't take the job to get rich."

He shook his head. "You're even more foolish than I thought."

She headbutted him, slamming her forehead into his nose. Pain rocked through her, but it was worth it to see blood trickling down his face. Hampered with her hands restrained, she still fought with everything she had, kicking him in the shins as hard as she could.

Fury filled his eyes. "That's going to cost you. I was going to make it as easy for you as possible, but…" He wiped blood from his nose. "This is on you," he said and hit her in the jaw.

She fell to her knees and bit back a sob, denying him the pleasure of hearing her cry out. Pride kept her eyes dry, so she simply raised her gaze and glared at him, hoping he could see the contempt she felt for him, but he wasn't done with her yet.

He reared back and kicked her in the stomach so that she rolled into the pit. "Enjoy your last minutes. And while you're at it, you might ask yourself where your high-and-mighty principles got you."

For the first time since he'd revealed his true colors, he smiled. It was a particularly scary look on him.

The breath knocked out of her, she simply lay on the ground for several minutes. Pain such as she'd never known poured through her. When she was able to think again, she figured she had a couple of broken ribs at the very least.

She breathed in and out in slow, measured breaths, trying to survive the nearly paralyzing agony. When she attempted to get to her feet, it was only to fall back down. Her knees took the brunt of her fall before she toppled sideways. This time, she was unable to hold back a sob.

Finally, she was able to get to her knees and from there to a standing position, not an easy feat with her hands tied behind her back. She picked her way across the rough ground and backed up to a footing. There, she rubbed her wrists back and forth against the wood, hoping to saw through the plastic. She felt the warm stickiness of blood as it dripped down her wrists.

Did she feel a little give in the plastic? Encouraged, she kept sawing until at last the shred of plastic dropped away. Now to get out of the pit. The sides were sheer with little to grab on to, but she managed to get a handhold and pulled herself up a couple of inches. She repeated the process until she was nearly at the top.

The roar of an engine alerted her that Brooks was making good on his threat. She stared in horror as the huge earthmover made its way toward her, and, startled, fell back into the pit.

Dirt rained down on her.

She stumbled her way to the far side of the pit. If this was to be her last few minutes, she didn't want to spend them being on the outs with the Lord. "Forgive me, Lord, for pushing You from my life. That was the wrong move. When Jeff died, I was so angry, so afraid, and I pushed You away just when I needed You most." She realized then that she had never stopped believing.

Not really. She'd just forgotten Him in her anger and her grief.

She waited, listening. There were no earth-shattering revelations or other signs that her prayer had been heard, only a quiet peace that stole over her like a gentle caress.

The relentless siege of dirt falling down on her didn't slow. If anything, it gained momentum. There was nowhere to run.

She wanted to feel courageous, resolute. She wanted to stand before Brooks without flinching, without showing even a hint of fear. She wanted to show that she could stand up to anything, but her stomach was cramping with the paralyzing fear of being buried alive.

When she'd been thirteen years old, she and Jeff had taken a picnic lunch to the foothills. After lunch, he'd stretched out on a blanket, and she'd decided to collect a bouquet of autumn leaves. The innocent act had resulted in near tragedy when she'd fallen through an abandoned mine shaft.

Her cries for help had finally reached Jeff, who fortunately had had an emergency kit in his truck, including a rope. He'd pulled her out, but she'd never forgotten the total darkness of being surrounded by earthen walls, or the terror of having those walls crumble around her as she'd struggled to climb them, her fingers scrabbling at the dirt. Though lumber had reinforced the walls when the mines had been in operation, time and insects had eaten away at the wood until little was left.

Was that like being covered with tons of loose dirt? Close enough.

The force of the unrelenting barrage of dirt knocked her down. She fought her way to standing and was knocked down again. Over and over she struggled to stand against the unremitting tide until she was certain she couldn't do it again.

One more time, she promised herself, and pushed to her feet. Again.

Rafe didn't delude himself. Brooks had a decent-size head start and a whole lot of desperation on his side. All Rafe had was a bunch of *ifs*.

If Rafe was right about Brooks taking Shannon to one of Calhoun's construction sites. *If* he was right as to which site he'd thought the most likely. Too many *ifs*. *Ifs* could get somebody killed. But *ifs* were all he had.

He drove to the site he'd pinpointed. If he was wrong… He didn't finish the thought. He couldn't afford to go there. Shannon was counting on him.

As he neared the site, the pavement vanished. He careened onto a dirt road, hit a pothole that could have doubled for a swimming pool, given the recent rains, and came out on the other side with a thump that jarred him down to his bones. He grunted along with the truck but barely slowed down. Couldn't afford to.

He flattened the gas pedal to the floor, hurtling the vehicle forward. When he reached his destination, he parked outside the site, not wanting to alert anyone to his presence, and hiked through a maze of pallets stacked with joists and rebar. When he spied two men hefting hammers, probably lookouts, he slowed. He recognized one as the man who had escaped after attacking Rafe and Shannon outside her office building.

Before he could duck behind a pallet, the men turned. A toothy grin appeared on one man's face. He said something to his partner then advanced upon Rafe.

Rafe didn't wait for the man to reach him, but moved in. He gave a quick, hard jab to the man's jaw and followed up with a short-armed punch to the solar plexus. He hadn't figured on the other guy coming from behind. Pain crawled up his injured arm. He did his best to ignore it. He couldn't give in to it, not when Shannon's life was at stake.

The second man wrapped his arm around Rafe's neck and tried to force his head backward. Ligaments in Rafe's spine began to yowl and buckle under the strain.

He rammed his elbow into his foe's gut. While he struggled for air, Rafe spun him around and slammed the man against a stack of iron fittings, the thrust lifting him off the ground. His opponent fell down heavily.

The first man wasn't done and came at Rafe again. He wrapped thick arms around Rafe's middle, squeezing him until Rafe felt like a rapidly deflating balloon. Just when he was certain he was going to pass out from lack of oxygen, he reared back his head and banged it into his enemy's forehead. The force knocked the man back, causing him to release Rafe and stumble to the ground.

But he wasn't finished.

He grabbed Rafe around the ankles and pulled him down. Momentarily stunned, Rafe took an instant to catch his breath. That moment cost him as the man pounced on him. They wrestled there on the dusty slab of concrete, until, with a mighty effort, Rafe threw the man from him.

He spent several seconds securing the two men's hands behind their back with zip ties, but it appeared he wasn't done. Not yet.

When he turned, it was to find Brooks holding a nine mil on him, a smarmy smile on his face. "Isn't this charming? The bodyguard rides to the rescue."

"Where's Shannon?"

"You're too late."

"For your sake, you'd better hope that you're wrong." Rafe swept his leg in a wide arc and kicked the weapon from Brooks's hand. He then folded his fingers under his knuckles and rammed the hard ridge of bone into the soft cartilage of the man's Adam's apple, gratified to hear a harsh gasp of air forced from his lungs followed by a wet, gurgling sound. He spared a few precious moments securing Brooks's hands and feet.

The steady growl of an engine had him looking to his left, where he caught sight of a man operating a huge dump truck. Rafe rushed to the truck, yanked the man from the cab and pulled him out. He climbed in the truck and halted the action.

"Shannon? Shannon!"

"Here."

He ran toward the sound of her voice and saw her in a nearly full pit of dirt. He hunkered down on the edge, reached for her and pulled her up.

She fell against him and held on.

"It's all right," he murmured against her hair. "It's all right now. I've got you."

Rafe lifted her and carried her to his truck. There, he laid her on the back seat, more than a little concerned when he saw her eyes were closed. Had she passed out from the ordeal?

He reached for the bottle of water, poured a small amount on his handkerchief and smoothed it over her face. The bruise on her jaw had him folding his lips into a tight line. Brooks had a lot to answer for.

"Shannon. Come back to me."

To his intense relief, she stirred a little and opened her eyes. "Rafe?"

"I'm here."

"I knew you'd come." Her eyes closed once more.

He called 911. After making sure that Shannon was breathing all right, he retraced his steps and yanked Brooks up from the ground by grabbing a fistful of his shirt. Feet bound, the man could barely stand, so Rafe pushed him onto a bench.

"Consider yourself fortunate that Shannon is going to be all right. Otherwise, I can't promise that you'd come through this."

"You have no right—"

It took every bit of restraint Rafe had not to smash his fist into Brooks's face. "I have every right. You're a parasite. You're also a bully and a coward. I've had plenty of practice dealing with the likes of you. How do you feel about taking on someone your own size?"

Brooks started to say something else, but Rafe cut him off. "If you know what's good for you, you'll shut up."

Brooks must have had some sense of self-preservation for he kept quiet.

When the EMTs arrived, Rafe handed over Shannon with relief.

"We'll take care of her."

"Where're you taking her?" he thought to ask.

"Shadow Points General Hospital."

Rafe wanted to go to the hospital with her, but he knew Shannon would want him to make sure Brooks was taken into custody. The police showed up, and Rafe gave a brief explanation, then raced to the hospital.

He found Shannon's room and exhaled in relief when he saw her sitting up and looking far better than she had a scant hour earlier.

He crossed the room and skimmed a hand across her cheek. He then fished the gold chain from his pocket and fastened it around her neck. It had taken a few minutes to repair the broken link, but he'd managed. "Thought you might want this back."

She fingered the delicate piece of jewelry. "Thank you."

He shared with her what he'd learned about the connection between Newton and Brooks and Calhoun.

"It makes sense," she said slowly, "that Brooks and Calhoun would turn to someone like Newton to do their dirty work."

She received a call and listened, a satisfied look appearing in her eyes. "Thanks for calling,

Detective. I appreciate it." She turned to Rafe. "That was Lannigan. Brooks is talking. Lannigan says they can't shut him up. Blaming it all on Calhoun. No surprise there." Her lips tipped in a faint smile. "He also asked that I pass along his apologies to you." She bent over her phone and typed furiously.

A few minutes later, she looked up from where she had been working at her cell. "I'm having a warrant sent to my phone. I want to see his face when we tell him it's over," she said. "Don't worry. We'll have black-and-whites with us."

He was worried, but not about taking down Calhoun—he was concerned about Shannon. She looked delicate enough to break apart at the least touch. After what Brooks had put her through, she needed rest and coddling. What she really needed was to stay in the hospital, but he knew that wasn't going to fly.

"Are you with me?" she asked.

"Always." Shannon wouldn't be dissuaded from making the trip to be there for Calhoun's arrest. Rafe hadn't expected anything different, and exchanged exasperated looks with the doctor. He waited for Shannon to dress, then helped her into the truck as carefully as though she was made of fine porcelain and drove to Calhoun's office.

It was mid-evening, but Rafe figured that the

odds were good of finding Calhoun at his office. A man like that was probably a workaholic.

When the security guard tried to stop Shannon and him, he pointed to the officers accompanying them. "Is Calhoun in?"

The guard nodded.

"Unless you want trouble, don't call ahead."

As they entered his office, Calhoun looked up, his expression slightly alarmed, before it altered to a practiced smile. When Rafe looked closer, though, he saw the twitching at the corners of Calhoun's eyes, belying the confidence his smile was designed to show.

"What can I do for you folks?" Calhoun asked genially. "Do you have more questions?"

"Just one," Shannon said. "How do you feel about prison orange?"

He stood and loomed over his desk, his stance designed to intimidate. "Is this some kind of joke?"

"No joke." She gestured to the two uniforms behind her. "These fine officers are here to inform you that you're under arrest."

"For what?" he demanded.

"For starters, murder. Attempted murder. Intimidation. Bribery of an elected official."

"And for being a morally bankrupt, lowlife scumbag," Rafe added for good measure.

Not by so much as by a blink of the eye did

Calhoun betray any nervousness. "Brooks will see to it that you never get a warrant."

Shannon gave him a hard smile. "We've got you cold, Calhoun. Including witness testimony. Once the forensic accountants get a look at your books, I'm sure they'll find even more evidence."

Shannon pulled up the warrant on her phone and showed it to him. "Already have one. As for Brooks, didn't I tell you? He's already in custody. He may be in booking by now." She sent an inquiring look to Rafe. "Did I forget to mention that?"

"You've had a lot on your mind." He turned a bland smile on Calhoun. "You understand, I'm sure."

"Of course, he understands," Shannon said. "He's a smart man. So smart that he knows he's going to spend the next twenty years or more in the slammer."

Calhoun scowled at her. "You think you're funny. We'll see how funny you're feeling when I sue you for false arrest."

"False arrest? I don't think so. The last I heard about Brooks, he was already rolling over on you." She looked at Rafe. "What do you think? Will he protect his good buddy or will he sing like the proverbial canary?"

"My money's on the canary," he said.

Shannon turned back to Calhoun. "Of course, you know him best. What do you think he'll do?"

The sour look on Calhoun's face told its own story.

"Take him in," she said to the officers, who hadn't said anything as they'd waited. "Oh, and be sure to read him his rights. We want to do this strictly by the book. After all, Mr. Calhoun is a very important person, as he will no doubt tell you."

"I'll be out before you file your paperwork," Calhoun boasted, but the desperation in his eyes negated the words.

"You go right ahead and think that," Shannon said. "It may help you get through the next few hours, but it won't change anything." She made a tsking sound. "I've heard that being booked can be rough, especially for someone like yourself, who is used to the finer things in life."

With a uniformed officer on each side of him, Calhoun alternately moaned and blustered, begged and threatened, as he was led out of his office.

She turned to Rafe. "We did it."

"You did it."

"We did it," she said.

The job was over. His reason for being with Shannon was over. Why did it feel like his reason for getting up in the morning was over, as well?

SEVENTEEN

The next five days passed in a blur. Statements to the police followed by more statements and testifying in front of a grand jury.

Outside the grand jury room, she faced her former boss without flinching.

"You're a fool," Brooks whispered as he was marched past her. "You think you've won, but you don't know what you're up against."

Calhoun didn't deign to speak to her, but the hate-filled scowl he shot her way had her grateful he was in restraints.

She didn't respond, only gave him a contemptuous glare and was relieved to see him taken away.

She hadn't seen Rafe much after they had both given their statements. She supposed he was busy with the paperwork in closing the case, but was he too busy to call or drop by to see her? When he showed up at her office that afternoon, it was all she could do not to run to him and wrap her arms around his neck.

Something in his expression stopped her.

"Hi." The one syllable was all she could manage.

"Hi, yourself."

She smiled self-consciously. "How've you been?" The inane question was accompanied by a flush of pleasure at seeing him. Her heart gave a hiccup of joy before settling, and she resisted the impulse to dip her head to hide the telltale color that she knew must have settled on her cheeks.

"Fine. You?"

"Fine."

The awkward conversation stretched into an even more awkward silence.

"With Brooks and Calhoun in jail, we have a good likelihood of bringing down the entire gang," she said, more in an attempt to fill the silence than to impart information. "By the way, Brooks gave up the woman who drugged me the night of the fundraiser. She worked for him, carrying payoff money back and forth between him and Newton and his gang."

"That's great." But his voice didn't back up what he'd said. The thick resonance implied he was having a hard time getting out the words. As though aware that he didn't sound pleased with the news, he added, "The city owes you a lot. You never gave up."

"I couldn't have done it without you."

"The DA's office is fortunate to have you," he said, sounding oddly formal. "Any word on who will take the top job?"

Why was he acting this way? And why were they talking about her job? As important as it was to have Calhoun and Brooks behind bars, it paled in comparison to what she wanted with Rafe.

"Not yet."

"Seems to me that you're the natural choice."

She shook her head. "No way. The job is too political for me. I'm not good at playing games with city hall. I'm happy right where I am."

"I'm not surprised."

"What about you?" she asked, relieved to leave the subject of herself. "What's next?"

"S&J will assign me another case. I like to stay busy."

"I hope your future client is more cooperative than your last one."

That raised a smile from him. "My last client was one in a million. I'm sorry to be saying goodbye to her." He stumbled over the last word.

Did he actually shuffle his feet? That wasn't like the confident man she'd come to know.

"Is that what you're doing? Saying goodbye?" *Please don't let it be true.*

"Yeah. I guess so. You're going to have your hands so full bringing the cases against Brooks and Calhoun to trial that you won't even miss me."

I already miss you.

It took all of her willpower not to ask "What about us?" But she kept the words inside and maintained her composure.

Rafe did something she'd never seen him do before. He shuffled his feet. Actually shuffled them, like an embarrassed schoolboy.

She had to put an end to this before she said something that she couldn't take back. Something like *I love you* and *I'll always love you. There will never be anyone else for me but you.* Something that would cause him to take pity on her and run as fast as he could in the opposite direction.

"Thank you. For everything." *Please say something*, she silently begged. *Please don't leave.*

"All part of the job."

Was that all she'd been? A job? She bit down on her lip before she cried out her pain. "Of course."

"Look, Shannon, I didn't mean—"

"I know what you meant. Stop in if you can spare the time." Though her heart was breaking into shards of unbearable pain, she made her tone one of casual dismissal. Every breath she drew sliced into her throat like chips of broken glass.

She longed to tell him everything that was in her heart, but she couldn't. Because somewhere deep inside, she was still that little girl with the bruised heart whose parents had abandoned her. Because she was afraid of being rejected again. Because she was too afraid to risk her heart a second time. Because she would once more wonder why she wasn't enough.

"Sure." The pain in his eyes made him look anything but sure.

The air was heavy with all that she wanted to say but couldn't, and all she longed to hear but didn't.

When the silence stretched to an unbearable length, she gave a pointed look at her desk. "If we're finished, I have a ton of work to do."

"Sure."

The man seemed to have a one-word vocabulary today.

"Goodbye, Rafe."

He turned on his heel and exited her office, closing the door quietly behind him.

But, to her heart, the sound of the door closing was anything but quiet. The noise reverberated down to her soul.

Why had he even stopped by? Was it to let her know that they didn't have a future together? If so, he could have told her outright instead of letting her almost make a fool of herself by telling him that she loved him and always would.

She propped her elbows on her desk and bowed her head into her hands. How could she have so wrong in interpreting his feelings for her? Had she been so eager to find love that she'd mistaken his concern for her safety for more than what it was?

Feelings, she reminded herself, couldn't be trusted. She and Rafe had shared life-threatening experiences. Had fear and gratitude masqueraded as something more?

No! What she felt for him was the real thing.

First her parents had deserted her, then her fiancé, and now Rafe. She was alone again. Her life was empty, with loneliness rushing in to fill the vacant places.

No. That was wrong. The belief she'd so recently reclaimed reminded her that she wasn't alone. Not anymore.

She bowed her head. "Lord, I could really use Your help right along now."

How long she stayed that way, she couldn't have said. A minute? Five? More?

When she felt strong enough, she lifted her head. *Enough.* She wouldn't waste another minute feeling sorry for herself.

Her motions precise, she straightened the files on her desk and set about making sense of the next case on her ever-growing to-do list. Work didn't care if her heart was shattered.

Getting to the core of the case against a man who had embezzled from his own company and cheated the stockholders kept her mind occupied. He had brazenly stolen funds and hidden them in accounts spread across the West. Though she didn't have any formal training in forensic accounting, she understood the principles well enough to follow the money trail.

After two hours, she had a firm grip on the case and was ready to make her recommendations. The satisfaction she experienced upon untangling the web of fraud and deceit felt good.

It was too bad it couldn't fill the emptiness in her heart, as well.

Rafe called himself all kinds of a fool as he left the building and walked to his car. He'd messed up. What had he been thinking? Telling Shannon that what he'd done was all part of the job? He'd seen the stricken look in her eyes, though she'd done her best to hide it.

For long minutes, he thought about going back and fixing what he'd broken, but he was too much of a coward to do so. If anyone else had called him a coward, he'd have come up fighting, but that's exactly what he was. A coward, too terrified to tell the woman he loved that he wanted to spend the rest of his life with her. All because he didn't know how to give his trust.

He'd told himself if he saw Shannon once more that he could close the door on his feelings for her. How wrong he'd been.

Now he had to live with it.

He didn't return to S&J immediately. He needed time to adjust to the knowledge that he didn't have a future with Shannon. Or with any woman. He'd been a fool to think he had.

He wasn't shallow enough to believe that his missing leg was reason to end a relationship. It went far deeper than that, into the dark recesses of his heart and soul. When Victoria had confessed that she'd cheated on him while he was deployed, something inside him had died.

Trust.

In his line of work, trust didn't come easy. He'd trusted his Delta brothers and, more recently, his colleagues at S&J including some outstanding women operatives. But giving his heart to a woman was a different matter. He wasn't sure he'd ever be ready to put his trust in another woman, not even Shannon.

What he'd felt for Victoria paled in comparison to his feelings for Shannon. She was light and breath to him. Though he couldn't picture Shannon cheating on anyone, he knew he needed to be able to trust again before he could make a real commitment.

"Get it together, Zuniga," he muttered to himself.

Shannon was a strong woman and would go on with her life, just as he would. The pep talk fell flat, though, as he acknowledged that it didn't feel like much of a life without her in it. By the time he made it to the S&J office, he had come to terms with his reality.

Seeing Shelley Rabb Judd there took him aback. "I didn't expect to see the boss," he said. "What brings you here to Colorado?"

"I decided to pay the Denver office a visit." She gave him a critical look. "Looking a little rough around the edges."

He pushed out a smile that felt as forced as it probably looked. "Thanks, boss. Just what I needed to hear."

"You did a good job on the DeFord case. There'll be a bonus in the next paycheck."

"No." The word exploded from him. The last thing he wanted was a bonus for guarding the woman he loved beyond reason. At Shelley's curious look, he said, "I mean, I don't need a bonus for doing my job."

"Did something happen while you were doing that job?"

"The usual stuff." He tried for an off-hand

tone. Judging by the expression in Shelley's eyes, he'd failed. Miserably. He prayed she'd leave it alone.

"Oh. I see."

He was afraid she did see. His boss could be uncannily perceptive.

"Are you ready for another assignment?" she asked. "Or do you want some time off? You're due for a vacation pretty soon."

Could she tell that he was nearly salivating for something to sink his teeth into?

"I'm up for a new job. What do you have?"

"A software company wants to up their security measures in their Denver headquarters. You'd be responsible for finding the weaknesses and plugging them, then making suggestions. Should be right up your alley."

"Piece of cake."

"That's what I thought." Another quizzical gaze. "You're sure you're all right?"

"Fine." The clipped word came out sounding rude. "Thanks."

"You want to talk, I'm available."

He knew she meant it. Shelley was a hard-headed businesswoman who could out-negotiate a top negotiator and take down a man twice her size with only her bare hands, but she was also a good friend. If he took her up on her offer, he knew she'd get the truth out of him. The last thing he wanted was to be an object of pity.

After murmuring a hasty goodbye, he couldn't get out of the office fast enough and headed home, but there was no comfort to be found there. Well, what had he expected? His life revolved around work. There was no one to come home to. His mother and sisters cared about him, loved him, but it wasn't the same as having a wife, a family of his own.

The hours after work were spent alone. Rafe welcomed the solitude. Or so he told himself. But after a few days, the aloneness pressed down upon him and became oppressive. He did his best to shake it off, but it clung like a burr and wouldn't release him from its grip.

Loneliness morphed into a festering wound. Instead of seeking out the company of friends, he roamed around his house, searching for something, anything, to do. He ended up cleaning every surface and wall until everything shone and he was left with nothing else to do.

The activity had exhausted his physical self, but the emotional pain was still alive and felt dangerously like the depression he'd experienced in the early days of rehab as he struggled to learn to walk with a prosthetic leg. No way did he want to go through that bleak period again, when he'd been certain his insides were as damaged as the outside.

The cat he'd unofficially adopted wound his way around Rafe's legs. He'd found the orange tom slinking through the alley behind the bungalow. Half-starved and wild-looking, the cat had given Rafe a disdainful sniff until he had returned with a can of tuna. Gus, a name Rafe had later bestowed, had gobbled it up as if he hadn't eaten in weeks, which was probably not too far from the truth.

From there, he had come around every evening until Rafe had gauged the time right to bring him inside, feed him in the kitchen and give him a much-needed bath. They still bore the scars from that.

"We're all we've got," he said, as much to himself as to the big tom. "We'd best make the best of it."

Gus meowed, whether in agreement or protest, Rafe wasn't sure.

He remembered the promise he'd made his mother to stop by the house. It had nagged at him, but he'd loathed the idea of subjecting his family to the misery that followed him around like a malevolent shadow.

He made the twisting drive to the family home, which was set in the foothills—it was short in distance but long in memories. Most were pleasant, save for the last time he'd visited and been beseeched by his mother to take over Allcott Mining. Today, he found her in the breakfast room, working on a crossword puzzle.

"Raphael. It's so good to see you." She stood back, surveyed him with a mother's knowing eye. "You look lower than a snake's belly."

That surprised a laugh out of him. He'd never heard those words from his genteel mother. "Where did you come up with that?"

She smiled. "There's a lot you don't know about your mother. Including the fact that she taught middle school back before you were born. Before your father made his first fortune. Those kids taught me a lot, including 'snake's belly.'"

"Why am I just now hearing about this?"

She clasped, then unclasped her hands. "There was a time when I wanted you and your sisters to think that we were born into money." A frown worked its way across her lips before she continued. "I wonder why that mattered. The truth is that your father and I subsisted on rice and beans for several years. To make ends meet, I taught school and clipped coupons while your father dug ditches and spun dreams." She lifted a slender shoulder. "Eventually those dreams came true."

"Did you believe we'd think less of you if we knew how you started?"

She gave a sheepish laugh. "I guess I was

projecting my parents, which was foolish of me. They wanted me to marry into the right family and become a privileged woman who never had to lift a finger, as my mother had been. They were violently opposed to my marrying your father. They wanted something better for me, never realizing that he was the best man I ever knew. Eventually they came around, but it took years."

Rafe processed what he was hearing. A lot of things made sense now, like the strained relationship between his grandparents and his father, one that had really never gotten any better. Even at a young age, he understood that his grandparents and father hadn't liked each other, as evidenced by the tense "company" manners that everyone used when his mother's parents came to visit.

"I promised myself I'd never behave as my parents did, but I let foolish pride take over in wanting you to run the business. Now I realize that it almost cost me my son." Her voice was throaty while tears glistened in her eyes. She pulled a monogrammed handkerchief from the pocket of her slacks and dabbed at her eyes. "I'm proud of the work you do, Raphael. I've always been proud."

"Thank you." Wasn't that what Shannon had told him? He should have listened. Had he allowed the conflict with his mother to cloud his thinking? Was that part of the reason he'd broken things off with Shannon? A hundred times, a thousand times, he'd been tempted to call her, to beg her to forgive him. The expression in her eyes when he'd left her—somewhere between hope and heartbreak—remained seared in his memory.

"Can you forgive me?" his mother asked, drawing him back to the present.

"There's nothing to forgive." He pressed a kiss to her damp cheek.

She patted the seat beside her. "Tell me more about that lovely girl I saw you with at the fundraiser."

"She was a client."

"I have eyes. What I saw in yours that night was not business."

"It doesn't matter. The job's over."

Disappointment filled his mother's eyes. "That's not what I asked." She didn't give him an opportunity to respond. "I hope you're not going to let what happened with Victoria influence you. She was never good enough for you." Her eyes flashed with the protective instincts of a mother defending her young. "What about Shannon?" his mother asked.

He stared at her in surprise. "You remembered her name?"

"Of course I did. She was important to you and therefore she's important to me."

Talking with his mother about his feelings for a woman had him wanting to run in the opposite direction, and he resisted the urge to squirm under the steady gaze she leveled at him.

"Do you still have feelings for Victoria?"

Shocked, he could only shake his head. "No." Those feelings had long since died.

"Are you still hurting over her cheating on you while you were overseas?"

Was that it? "I don't know," he said honestly. "I know Shannon's not like that, but the whole trust thing keeps getting in the way."

His mother eyed him with a shrewdness that many a Delta commander would have envied. "Is that why you've pulled away from her?"

"How do you know I pulled away?" He heard the annoyance in his voice and dipped his head in apology. Right now he wasn't feeling certain about anything, but one thing he was sure about was that he needed Shannon in his life. "Sorry. I didn't mean to snap at you."

"Your eyes tell me so."

"How did you get to be so smart?" The question was part admiration, part irritation.

"I'm a mother."

EIGHTEEN

Shannon didn't have time to brood. At least not much. If she occasionally lapsed into wondering what-might-have-been with Rafe, she pulled herself out of it.

Mostly.

She had two cases to prepare for trial, both of them prosecutor's dreams, the kind that could make a career if handled properly. Now she had only to make the cases shine as examples showing that no one, not even a district attorney, was above the law.

Brooks and Calhoun couldn't wait to roll over on each other. It was almost comical seeing them trying to outdo the other in turning state's evidence. So much for loyalty among crooks.

Even though she didn't mind the long hours and enjoyed the process of putting together a case, she wished she had someone to come home to at the end of the day, someone with whom to share the ups and downs.

"Are you working late again?" Georgia asked, concern in her eyes.

Shannon nodded, barely looking up. She had statements to review, case law to bone up on and opening arguments to prepare for in what were probably the most important cases of her career. "'Fraid so."

"You don't have to do everything all by yourself," the secretary said.

Shannon gave her a grateful smile. "Thanks. I'll be heading home soon."

With a doubtful look, Georgia said goodbye.

Touched by her concern, Shannon promised herself that she'd keep her word and close up shop soon. In the meantime, her stomach was making rumbling noises, reminding her that she'd skipped lunch. Again. Maybe she could squeeze in a trip to the vending machine and get a sandwich. Even stale ham-and-cheese sounded good right along now.

The workload didn't bother her. If anything, it made the long nights easier to get through.

Why should her loneliness bother her now? She was accustomed to being alone. But that was before Rafe had found his way into her life.

She wasn't lonely for just anyone. She was lonely for him.

She shoved away that thought and reminded herself that things were good. Her career was on track. The new DA was a woman she both liked and respected. With the information she and the police had amassed from Brooks and Calhoun, they'd identified three other towns that crews similar to Newton's had been terrorizing. Unsurprisingly, the leaders and lieutenants of the crews all had snakes tattooed on their arms. Mrs. Kimball was going to make a full recovery. It would be a long haul, but she had one of the best doctors in the West attending her. Dani Rabb had convinced one of her father's friends, a highly regarded neurosurgeon who was based in the Midwest, to take the case pro bono.

Best of all, Shannon had welcomed the Lord back into her life and now recognized His hand in so many things. Never again would she doubt His goodness or His love for His children, including herself.

Yes, everything was going great. Except that her heart was shattered. Rafe's absence from her life was an ache that consumed her every fiber, and she missed him like her own heartbeat.

Pain has a flavor, she'd decided long ago. When her parents had left her with scarcely a goodbye, it had tasted like applesauce, the last food her mother had given her. Now, with Rafe's desertion, it tasted of stale sandwiches and pop, the meals he'd insisted she eat when she couldn't make time for anything else. Would she ever be able to grab anything from the vending machine again without thinking of him?

There was a time, not that long ago, when she'd dreamed of marriage and children, a family like the one she hadn't had. Children's voices would fill the rooms, along with laughter and teasing and enough clutter to make the house a home. A big foolish dog with a sweet face and a cat who was always underfoot would complete the picture.

That dream had died when her fiancé had deserted her, but it had reawakened when Rafe had walked into her life.

Get over it.

Rafe was gone. She wouldn't humiliate herself by begging him to love her as she loved him. She'd shared with him in ways she'd never thought to do with anyone, trusting him with one of her most closely guarded secrets—the pain of her parents' abandonment. And though she hadn't actually said the words aloud, she'd allowed him to see her sorrow.

It hadn't made a difference. He still hadn't been willing to trust her with his heart.

Despite the self-directed lecture that they didn't belong together, longing bloomed in her heart, a song of rising joy when Rafe showed up unexpectedly in her office. To hold it close, she placed her hands on her chest and savored the sensation. As quickly as it appeared, though, it was doused and replaced by a healthy dose of anger.

She refused to give in to either, refused to give him that much control over her. No more than a second later, two at the most, she assured herself, she put on her game face, even as a bright spot of pain twisted in her heart. Though her hands wanted to tremble, she kept them steady by an effort of will.

When Rafe showed up unexpectedly in her office, her belly tightened and clutched. Nerves wanted to bubble up, but she ruthlessly squelched them and schooled her face into a cool expression. "Did we have an appointment?" She pretended to check her calendar, though she knew there were no appointments for the evening.

"No. Do I need one?"

She made a point of shuffling some files. If she kept her hands busy, maybe she wouldn't notice the war that sorrow and love waged within her. "As you can imagine, I'm a little busy."

He perched on the corner of her desk. "Too busy to see a friend?"

"Is that what we are? Friends?"

"I hope so."

She wanted so much more, but she set aside the files she'd been hiding behind and looked up at him. "Why are you here, Rafe?"

"I had to see you."

"Why?"

"Be-e-cause…" The single word stretched out. He stood, paced the narrow length of the room and back again, this time taking a seat in the room's one visitor's chair.

She tilted her chin in challenge. "Not a good reason."

"You know why." His voice was so low that she could barely make out the words.

"No. I'm afraid I don't. I thought we'd finished any business we had between us when you walked out." She bit her lip in frustration. Not at Rafe, but at herself. She hadn't meant to add those last words. They revealed far too much, but it was too late to yank them back, and so she held his gaze without turning away.

The hurt in his eyes told her that her words had found their target. She felt small and mean and was about to apologize when he said, "Cheap shot."

She supposed she deserved that, but she hadn't deserved the hurt he'd inflicted by leaving without an explanation. "You're right. It was. So was walking out on me."

"It was unforgivable."

She stared at him in surprise. And her heart stuttered a bit as she saw the pain in his eyes.

"You think I don't know that?" he asked.

"That makes it worse."

"Yeah, it does. I don't have any defense for how I acted."

She ought to be grateful that he accepted that; instead, though, it only rubbed acid in the wound.

"Except one," he added. "I was running scared. Scared of my feelings for you. I'd never felt anything like that before."

"What about Victoria?"

It burned her that she remembered his ex-fiancée's name. It shouldn't have stuck in her mind as though it held any importance. As though *he* held any importance.

Rafe shook his head. "Whatever I once felt for her doesn't even compare to what I feel for you." His voice had thickened to a hoarse rasp.

She couldn't help it. She looked away, unable to face the raw feeling in his eyes. How long could she keep this up without falling apart? She looked down at her hands, which were rigid with tension. Slowly, deliberately, she relaxed them and shifted her gaze back to him.

She reminded herself that he was only the last in a line of people who had abandoned her. A tiny ache was tearing into her already wounded heart. When he left, she would do her best to repair it.

Sparring with him was taking a toll, and she looked for a way to end it. Feeling more in control as her hands unclenched, she lifted her gaze and met Rafe's. "If there's nothing else…" There. Casual and cool should do the trick, but her thoughts were anything but casual and her heart anything but cool.

Anger slid under love. She held on to the anger. If she gave way to the love, she feared she might do something supremely foolish, like kiss him with all the pent-up love she'd done her best to contain for the last two weeks.

She steeled herself against the call of her treacherous heart, even as it now tripped her into her throat. *You don't have the right to make me love you.* But she kept it to herself. She wouldn't give him another weapon.

The heat of anger had burned away, leaving her confused and empty and so lost. A hundred…no, a thousand thoughts crowded her mind, yet not one came through clearly.

"Whatever you thought you felt, you were wrong. Now I really must insist that you leave. I have work that won't wait."

Please go, she begged silently before the tears that were threatening spilled over and she humiliated herself before him.

Rafe had been prepared to face Shannon's anger, her tears, even her bitterness. He accepted that he deserved all three—and more—and promised himself he would deal with them with gentleness and love. He'd apologize for being a fool, beg her forgiveness and pray that she saw fit to let him back in her life.

What he hadn't been prepared for was cool indifference.

Had he miscalculated? Had he lost her forever with his pride and determination to be fair to her?

She hitched her chin to the mountain of files stacked on her desk, drawing his attention to her face. That face was one of uncompromising strength and enduring beauty, and it would out-last the years. He only prayed that he would be able to spend those years with her.

Relationships, he thought, were a puzzle, with an infinite number of ever-moving pieces, but, oh, how he wanted a forever one with Shannon. Marriage, with all its complications, the good and the bad, the highs and the lows.

"I'm sorry, Rafe. I really am buried with work. Perhaps another time…"

"No. Not another time."

Eyes flashing, she pushed back her chair and stood, her stance an unconscious one, he was certain, of combat. She paced the room, much as she'd done when she was working out a thorny problem on a case. She carried herself with pride, with dignity, with energy. In another time, an-other world, she would have been a warrior prin-cess, one who wore armor and carried a sword and shield. She was still a warrior, but her weapons were truth and justice that she wielded with courage and conviction.

Here, now, she was a woman who had trembled in his arms.

"Who do you think you are to come into my office, without an invitation I might add, and interrupt my work? Who gave you the right?"

The demand seared his soul.

"I'm the man who loves you!"

There. He'd said it. Let her dismiss that as she'd tried to dismiss him.

That must have gotten her attention, as she was rendered silent for a full minute. "Do you think that's all it takes? Saying those words? Love means trust. Love means commitment. Love means getting through the hard stuff and not walking out because you're scared." She didn't give him an opportunity to answer. "Did you love me when you walked out on me weeks ago? Did you love me when you told me that I was a job?"

And there was the snap of anger. Good. That meant she wasn't as indifferent to him as she'd pretended.

"That wasn't what I meant, and you know it."

"Do I? That's what you said."

"I didn't want to hurt you. I never wanted to hurt you." He shoved a hand through his hair. She had to know that he would never willingly hurt her. "I was trying to be fair to you."

"Is that what you call walking out on me? Being *fair*?" The word fairly crackled with energy and temper.

Her spine arrow-straight, she stared him down. It didn't matter that he topped her by more than a foot and outweighed her by a hundred pounds, he understood that she was the stronger of the two of them.

"You didn't let me finish."

"Let me do it for you. You judged me and found me guilty of being as shallow and selfish as your ex-fiancée."

Rafe kept his arms at his sides when all he wanted to do was to draw her into them and hold her and never let her go.

"You say you were doing it for me, but you were doing it for yourself. You were afraid. The big bad Delta was afraid." Anger still stained her face, but her expression had softened, and she laid a palm on his cheek. "If you can't be honest with me, at least be honest with yourself."

Gone was the anger. Gone was the dismissal. In their place was heart-breaking pain. He'd give anything to take away the sorrow he'd put in her eyes.

"You're right. I was afraid. But not for the reason you think." He drew in a long breath. "Before she broke up with me, Victoria told me that she'd cheated on me when I was overseas. It made me afraid to trust. Anyone. But especially myself. If I was wrong about her, what else was I wrong about?"

"Why didn't you tell me?"

"I don't know." But he was beginning to think that he did. Shannon and Victoria were both beautiful, both smart, both accomplished. Had he feared that Shannon was like his ex-fiancée in other ways?

With a start, he realized the truth: Shannon was nothing like Victoria. Why hadn't he understood that until now?

He had to get through to her that he meant every word when he'd told her that he loved her. It nearly broke him in half to admit that he might have tossed away what they could have together.

"You hurt me." And, with that, she withdrew her hand.

"I know." And himself. More than he could have ever realized. "I'm sorry for it. Sorrier than I can say." He took her hand and brought it back to his cheek, pressed it beneath his own.

When she didn't pull it away, a tender shoot of hope pushed up through the barren bleakness of the last two weeks.

"I love you," she said. "Nothing's going to change that, but I can't be with you if you can't trust me." She paused, letting it sink in. "Or yourself."

That's what it came down to. Trust. There couldn't be love without trust.

"Will you help me?" he asked with more humility than he'd ever asked for anything in his life.

"If you'll let me. You're the finest man I've ever known, Rafe. I want a life with you. A real life where we share everything, even the hard stuff. Especially the hard stuff."

He saw it then, the slightest twitch of her mouth as though her lips were fighting a losing battle not to lift in a smile. When they lost the battle and her smile bloomed full and complete, he felt as though he'd come home.

Everything that was important to him was held in the soft curve of her lips. Understanding. Compassion. Forgiveness. Love. Trust.

"I love you in every way a man can love a woman. As for the rest of it, I'll do my best to be there for you in whatever way you need, whatever way you want. I won't say that our lives will be perfect or that we'll never argue. We're both too strong-willed for that, but I will always love you."

"And I love you back. That's all that matters."

He saw it then, the dream he'd carried with him for as long as he could remember. A family of his own with love and laughter and even a few tears mixed together. "It is, isn't it?"

"Why did you stay away for so long?"

"Because I was a fool." He kissed her with all the love he'd foolishly held back.

"Don't ever leave me again." She raised to her toes and brushed a kiss across his lips. It was soft as rose petals yet powerful enough to send his mind reeling.

"I won't." He gathered her in his arms. "One thing, though."

She lifted an inquiring eyebrow.

"When you said the 'hard stuff,' does that mean you're taking me shopping with you again?"

She laughed softly. "Count on it."

* * * * *

*If you enjoyed this story, don't
miss Jane M. Choate's next
thrilling romantic suspense,
available later this year from
Love Inspired Suspense!*

*Find more great reads at
www.LoveInspired.com*

Dear Reader,

Thank you for joining me on Rafe and Shannon's love journey. As is true for many of us, their journey did not run smoothly. They hit bumps and snags, not to mention people trying to kill them! But they didn't give up. Even when things looked bleakest, they kept going.

That is my message here: keep going. Whatever challenges you face, whatever trials this mortal life throws at you, whatever betrayals you endure, keep going. The Savior is rooting for you. He has your back. He will not desert you. He will not abandon you. He loves you, as I tell my grandchildren, "to infinity and back."

With gratitude for His goodness,
Jane